CONTENTS

CHAPTER ONE

I'm Not Jealous But...

It was difficult not to envy the fairy tale my best friend had found herself the centre of.

I did envy her, but not enough to call it full blown jealousy. I might have been jealous, if Claudine and Matthew weren't so damn perfect for one another. I didn't know any two people who deserved their fairy tale as much as those two.

I was the first to enter the room in which the wedding breakfast would be held. Dena, that's Claudine - she went by Dena to her closest friends and family - had asked me to take her bouquet through and place it next to the cake. An important job apparently. One she couldn't entrust to any of her six bridesmaids.

I had not made the cut.

I understood why, I'd been upset of course, but I'd chosen to keep my mouth shut. The decision must have been hard enough for my best friend as it was, without me kicking up a stink. Claudine's husband was the eldest of five children and he was the only boy. So, his four younger sisters and baby niece had to be asked. Claudine had a sister also. She'd felt terrible when she told me she just couldn't have a seventh bridesmaid it would be too much.

It still felt like a kick in the teeth though.

Dena was one of my oldest friends. I could probably say my only true friend. Most definitely my best friend. We'd met twelve years ago, when we moved into the same student halls. We happened to be on the same course (music production) and our rooms were right next door. We liked the same music, the same films, we even had the same taste in boys. We'd very quickly become inseparable, and it had been that way over since. I would even go as far as to say I was closer to Dena than I was my own brother, or even my parents. She was more than just a friend. I considered her family.

Upon entering the room, I had to take a moment, just to catch my breath. It was called The Conservatory. That's just what it was, a large open plan room, with windows on every wall, bathing the whitewashed room in natural light. Ten round tables, each set up to seat eight guests complimented the room, with pristine white table cloths, white chairs, and in the centre of each table a tall candelabra, entwined with ivy.

It was so utterly perfect. Claudine had spent the last twelve months talking my ear off about the venue – an old hunting lodge turned hotel in the West Sussex Countryside, the centrepieces, the favours – a little corked bottle filled with a blend of tea the couple had dried and blended themselves, but nothing had prepared me for the reality, it really was like something straight out of one of those wedding magazines.

Eventually I gathered myself, walked around the edge of the room and placed the bouquet on the table next to the beautiful three tier cake, admiring it for a second. Then I was quickly snapped out of my little moment of thought by the bustle of other wedding guests starting to enter the room. Murmurs of approval drifted through the air as they also took in how utterly magnificent the space was.

This was the bit I'd been dreading. Almost one hundred guests and I only knew a handful. The bride and groom and their respective parents and siblings. But Matt had a big family, and Dena's family were very traditional, even if she was not. They'd insisted on every last cousin, great aunt and even her uncle's ex-wife and her new husband being invited. Although as Dena had pointed out, her parents were paying for everything, so she had to allow her lovely, but slightly overbearing mother some say over the guestlist.

But I was alone and was about the spend the next few hours of my life seated at a table of strangers, attempting to make polite conversation. Or the slightly worse alternative, nodding politely and forcing an optimistic giggle as Dena's Great Granny insisted it would me next, and the right man (Or woman 'you youngsters are open to anything these days') was right around the corner. As happy as I was for Dena and Matt, and how, deep down, I knew their nuptials would not make any difference to the dynamic of our friendship, it was a stark reminder, my best friend was now married, and I wasn't even close.

"Don't worry," Dena had assured me numerous times in the weeks leading up to the big day, "I've got a surprise for you. He's sitting next to you and he's hot."

That was all Claudine would give me on the subject. But it was always accompanied by a smug grin, and a reminder that they had gifted me with the Honeymoon Suite for the night, as they'd be leaving for their fortnight in Mexico before midnight. And she was fully expecting me to use it.

Dena tried not to make a big deal out of it, but she didn't keep it a secret that she was desperate for me to meet someone. I'd become single not long after she and Matt had gotten engaged and I knew she was very aware that her getting married was a constant reminder of my failed relationship. Although as I often reminded her, it had never been on the cards for me and my ex anyway. But I was still nursing somewhat of a broken heart.

It had been a year since my own happy ever after had come to an abrupt not so ever after. I'd handled the whole situation quite well, I thought. I'd moped and cried for an appropriate length of time. I'd spent a month in Dena and Matt's guest room, at Dena's insistence, allowing them both to spoil me with takeaways and ice cream to help ease the pain. Then I made the decision to move back to my Mum and Dad's whilst I got myself fully back on my feet. I'd dived headfirst into my work, and been so busy that before I knew it, it was twelve months down the line and I was still there. It was only recently that I'd started taking flat hunting a bit more seriously, and had some viewings lined up in the coming week.

I wasn't sure if I wanted another relationship. I absolutely was not ready for one. But these sorts of occasions were much easier to deal with when you had a plus one.

I'd checked the table plan before I'd entered the room and found my table quickly, locating my place card and setting my sparkly black clutch bag down next to the cutlery. I instantly regret-ted not taking note of who I'd be seated with. My hand curled around the back of the chair I still stood behind and I peered to the place setting to my left. The little card sitting next to the fa-vour read 'Thomas' in beautifully twisted calligraphy.

Oh, well it sounded like a nice normal name at least. I'd never met any weird Thomas'. Although Dena was prolific for setting me up with creeps who she insisted were lovely people. She saw the good in everyone. I was a little more...guarded. But Dena would describe me as unfairly judgemental which was why she and Matt were my only friends. That wasn't strictly true, I had lots of friends, but I just preferred their company above others.

Sighing, I pulled out the chair and settled myself down. *Stop being so morose this is your best friend's wedding day.* I told myself firmly.

With a new found determination to at least try and enjoy what was bound to be a tedious couple of hours, I plastered a smile on and delved into my clutch bag for my lipstick and compact. I quickly reapplied my red lipstick and checked the rest of my make-up was still intact.

"Fuck!" The expletive slipped out, as I fiddled to put the lid back on the makeup and it slipped from my fingers, hit the floor and rolled under the table out of my sight. "Oh, bloody hell," I muttered under my breath, scooting back and slipping from my chair, onto my knees and ducking beneath the table.

"Are you alright down there?" the sudden intrusion of a male voice and a pair of seemingly endless navy clad legs to my left, made me jump as I shuffled out. I straightened my back a little too quickly, managing to hit my head on the edge of the table.

"Ouch... yes... fuck," I didn't look in the direction of the voice, until I'd scrambled back up, and into a standing position next to my seat. Then I turned to the cause of the now throbbing spot on the top of my head, and waved my retrieved lid, "Dropped this."

I took a second to drink in the very tall glass of water now standing before me. How had I missed this guy at the ceremony and drinks reception? Standing tall, at well over six foot, and kitted out in the most perfectly tailored navy suit, teamed with white shirt, and co-ordinated burgundy tie and pocket square, he stood out that was for sure. Looks wise, he just had to be one of Matt's doctor friends, he had a professional air about him.

Just the way he held himself. He reached up and pushed his thick rimmed glasses up his patrician nose, with his middle finger and his hand continued its journey up to ruffle through his slightly too long auburn curls. Wow.

"I'm so sorry, I didn't mean to startle you, I'm Tom," the hand which was in his hair moments before was now stuck out before him, and I quickly accepted the gesture with the hand that was not occupied with the escapee lipstick lid. "I think this is me," he let go and gestured to the chair to my left.

"Great!" *okay, calm down*, "I'm Ada!" *really, Ada, calm yourself*. He wasn't my usual type, and I most definitely did have a type. But there was something about this man, and his elegant poise, and charming gestures which had me practically swooning. Dena had done good!

"Nice to meet you Ada," Tom smiled and we both sat at the table, just as another couple joined us along with two young girls. These people I recognised to be Dena's Aunt and Uncle, and her much younger cousins, I'd met them at a handful of occasions. I waved across the table and said hello. Before Tom drew my attention back, "So how do you know Matt and Claudine?"

"Oh well I-" but I was cut short by a thud on the table as a pint of beer was set down right by my place setting by a hand, joined to a heavily tattooed arm, with rolled up shirtsleeve… belonging to another man. My eyes widened, this guy was clearly the one Dena had in mind for me.

"Alright, I'm Dave, looks like I'm with you," Dave was probably just above average height, but it was difficult to tell from my seated position and he was quite broad. But with his tattoos, thick dark beard, and quiffed hair, he was most definitely my type. Clearly, I was his as well, because he completely ignored Tom and as he dragged out his chair and sat down. I watched his eyes travel down from my face, linger my chest for longer than necessary, then almost regrettably pull back up to my face, and he grinned a lecherous grin, "Lucky me."

This was the problem with 'my type' of man. They were usually arrogant sleazes and I could never learn to look past basic attraction and simply get to know someone first. Luckily this time, Tom was on my left to balance out the equation and remind me that there was a much better option.

Bless Tom, he must have sensed my awkwardness at our new tablemate's approach, as he interrupted our exchange, by leaning across me and sticking out his hand.

"Doctor Thomas Cambridge, pleasure," Dave accepted the handshake, whilst nodding and lifting his pint to his lips with his free hand.

"Doctor of what mate?" the question came, right before another slurp.

"Cardiology at Kings College."

"You must have gone to Medical School with Matt?" I piped up, pleased my initial assumption of his occupation and relation to the couple was correct.

"That's right."

"Neat, I was in a band with Matty when we were at college, best mates since we were five," strange, Matt had never mentioned a best friend called Dave. No one called him Matty either, except Dena when she was drunk and feeling soppy. "What about you Sweets," *Oh me?*

"I'm Ada, I went to Uni with Dena, we used to live together..." I was playing it down.

"I've heard about you," it was Tom, and he was grinning now, like he was privy to an inside joke, "By all accounts you two are mostly joined at the hip," I smiled fondly and nodded. Then Dave was interrupting.

"Oh shit, you're *that* Ada... Adelaide B, the DJ," I inwardly groaned. *Here we go.*

"Sound engineer," I corrected him.

"But you used to be a DJ?" Dave pressed.

"A long time ago," I didn't want to have this conversation, not because I was embarrassed about my younger years on the decks, but more because it quite often overshadowed my current career, which I'd worked hard for. As if by some saving grace, someone new joined our table and Dave couldn't get another word out.

"There you are, Tom," in a very swift but smooth action, Tom stood from his chair and had the chair next to him pulled out ready for the very beautiful, and very pregnant woman to sit down. "I'm sorry that took me so long, it's a maze to find the bathroom in this place, I should have gone up to the room."

"I should have gone with you love, I'm sorry," I watched the exchange curiously. I should have known a man as seemingly nice as Tom, and attractive to boot, couldn't possibly be single.

"I'm pregnant, Tom, not an invalid, I can manage going to the bathroom on my own," she was American, but not loud or in your face, like most of the American's I'd met through work. She was softly spoken, and her lips formed a constant smile. She was also really quite stunning, with blonde hair falling in waves to her shoulders, big brown eyes, and skin which glowed (although that could have just been the pregnancy). They made a striking couple.

"I'm sorry everyone, this is Grace...Grace this is Dave another friend of Matt's and Ada, Claudine's best friend," Tom quickly introduced his partner to us.

"Oh Ada, I've heard all about you," Grace giggled, "Claudine was showing me photos of your little hen weekend in Prague, it looked like you had a blast."

"Oh!" I laughed a little. Dena hadn't wanted a hen do; so instead she opted for a girly weekend in Prague, just the two of us. We had indeed had a blast, "Yeah that was great," I couldn't help peer over the table at her protruding stomach, giving her cause to sit further back from the table than must have been comfortable. "How far along are you?"

She rested a hand over the top of her bump, "Thirty-six weeks... and six days."

"Oh god, you're literally about to drop!" my eyes widened, and I chanced a look at Tom, his eyes were fixed firmly on his girlfriend's face, complete with an utterly adoring gaze.

"At least there are plenty of doctors on hand should you go into sudden labour," I joked, and she laughed politely. She must have heard that one before, being with a doctor and all.

"Shit, I knew I'd seen you before as well," both Tom and Grace shot surprised looks at Dave's loud interruption, and it took me a second to realise he was talking to me again, "You're Magnus Elliasson from Nuclear Choice's girlfriend, I saw them live a few times on their last tour."

"Mags and I haven't been together for over a year," my answer was automatic, but I heard my voice stiffen and crack. Not because I was upset, but more that I was taken off guard. It had been so long since anyone had mentioned Mags to me. It was a reminder of how much my life had changed in the past twelve months. It was much quieter now.

"I'm sorry," I didn't expect the sincere sounding apology which fell from Dave's lips. "I had no idea, I feel like an idiot now," he'd done a good job of sounding like an idiot before that comment, but I laughed and shook my head.

"You weren't to know... you're a fan then? Of the band?" clearly the guy did have some good taste. Magnus might be my ex-boyfriend, but I'd always be one of his biggest fans. It was as much my music as it was his.

"Yeah they're decent," Dave took another few gulps of his beer, and I watched the muscles in his throat move as he chugged down the golden liquid. I really wasn't so sure about this man. Looking back around our now full table I noticed Tom and Grace talking quietly between themselves, they looked sweet, but not sickeningly so. I almost had to hold back a sigh as I watched Tom lean towards his girlfriend, tuck a stray strand of her blonde hair tenderly behind her ear and place a light kiss on her cheek, close to her lips.

Maybe it was a sign of my age, but suddenly the slightly drunk, tattooed hunk, with a cocky air, and great taste in music, to my right was not quite as appealing as he might have been to me ten years ago. What I wouldn't give to have a man look at me with the respect and adoration with which Tom looked at Grace.

The afternoon wore on, and I couldn't deny I was enjoying myself, although the wedding breakfast had continued to be a strained and awkward affair. Tom and Grace tried to make polite conversation. Tom seemed genuinely interested in my line of work and asked me a lot of questions. Grace asked of my friendship with Dena, and I was happy to talk about my friend. But it was all made very difficult by Dave butting in with his stupid, incessant statements, mostly about me, about my ex, and still annoyingly about me being a DJ. None of this was helped by his repeated trips to the bar for lager and getting steadily drunker and louder as the meal progressed. I'd given up correcting him, and the whole table could see it grating on my nerves. But I powered on nonetheless.

CHAPTER TWO

A Problem Shared…

I was relieved though when the meal was over, and everyone retired to the bar for the room turnaround to get ready for the evening reception. I took the opportunity to run up to the room, freshen up and take advantage of the complimentary champagne on ice, having a quiet glass alone on the balcony before I headed back down to the party.

I finally ended up in the tight embrace of my best friend.

"You look incredible, I know I told you this morning, but you do Dena, you look beautiful," I held both of her hands tightly in mine, and she was smiling so widely I was sure her face must have been hurting.

"Thank you, thank you," she squeaked, her big brown eyes danced with joy. "I can't believe it, I'm married, I'm Mrs Tate."

"That's going to be so weird getting used to," I chuckled, and pulled her in for a second hug, "Where's Mr Tate?"

"Oh, outside I think, catching up with friends, speaking of which, what do you think of Davey?" Dena asked with a sly wink.

"Erm..." I hesitated, before managing to force what I hoped looked like an appreciative grin, "He's alright."

"I've only met him a handful of times, but he and Matt go way back, school or something, some terrible band he used to sing in." Dena explained, waving her hand dismissively "Hot though, right?"

"You know me too well." I wasn't going to lay into her on her wedding day about sitting me next to that letch of a man. So I nudged her playfully and laughed. She looked pleased with her-self, and that was fine, then I noticed her expression change to an amused sort of smirk and she looked right by me.

"Speak of the devil and he shall appear." she mumbled under her breath as a firm hand fastened its self around my waist and I felt myself pulled into a solid body.

"There she is, Claudine you have the fittest friends." *Oh Christ. Is this guy for real?*

I faked an over the top, flustered giggle and patted his chest, before ducking out of his embrace, and taking Dena by the hand, "I hope you'll excuse us Dave, but my friend and I have some drinking to do!" and I tugged Dena unceremoniously away to the bar, with her cackling in my wake.

The dancing later that night was great. I may no longer be a DJ, but I do have connections and Calum, an old friend from my club days in London had happily agreed to supply the music for the night. Between catch ups with him, and dancing with Dena, the night was turning out to be a belter. Even if I did have to con-tinuously avert creepy Dave's advances. Towards the end of the evening Matt had dragged me up for a soppy slow dance, drunk-enly whispering in my ear what an amazing friend I was to Dena and how he didn't know what either of them would do without me. Dena was my best friend first and foremost, but I'd known Matt for half as long, and he was just as special to me as she was. It was emotional, and by the time the taxi pulled away from the hotel at just gone half past ten, taking the newlyweds to the airport, I was having to furiously bat tears away from my eyes.

The moment overwhelmed me as I stepped back inside, and from the corner of my eye I could see Dave swaying slightly at the function room bar. He was looking around and I knew he was trying to spot me through his drunken haze. I hurried across the room quickly and retrieved my bottle of Chablis from the table I'd commandeered for the evening, along with a glass and hotfooted it out to the gardens.

I wandered for a little, looking for a quiet place to hide myself. Finally, I settled myself on some stone steps which led down to a lake lit up by lights in the surrounding bushes. It was very pretty, and although still in sight of the main building, secluded. It was what I needed. I poured myself a glass of wine and brushed the last few tears from my eyes.

"You know, it's not healthy to drink alone," I'd been sitting alone for good fifteen minutes, and I jumped at the voice which came from behind above me, having not heard any footsteps across the grass. But I recognised that low cadence. I smiled up at Tom as he descended a couple of the steps and sat down beside me.

"Well I'm not alone am I? You're here." I sassed, and held out my glass to him, "I don't have the lurgy I promise." He accepted the glass and took a couple of generous sips before passing it back.

"I can't help but notice you're a little glum. Considering your best friend just got married and all," *I hadn't been that obvious, had I?*

"Oh no, I'm happy for her, just a bit emotional you know, saying goodbye. I know it's only a fortnight, but I don't think I've ever gone that long without seeing her. It's silly but I'm going to miss them," an eruption of jeers came from the building a few hundred feet away and I looked over my shoulder in a moment of panic.

"I just saw concierge shove him into a taxi, you're safe," *Rapid change of subject.*

"I'm sorry."

"Don't be, the guy was an unmitigated arse. My heart went out to you at dinner, it honestly did," I took another sip, and passed the glass back to Tom, finally looking at him properly. He grinned at me when I did. "So tell me, because I know there's more to it, than missing your friend. What's got you so blue?"

"You really don't want me to bore you with it," I sighed.

"I do," he picked up my bottle of wine and topped up the glass then handed it back to me.

"Really...you don't."

"I insist," he pressed, and I felt my resolve weakening. *What was it about this man that made me want to open my soul? I barely knew him.*

"Dena and Matt are so perfect together," I exhaled loudly and Tom nodded, but a slight frown told showed me his confusion as to where I was going. "They're so lucky. It's not the wedding, that's not what I'm sad about really and I'm not jealous, not at all. It was just a reminder of what I don't have...or what I did have, but don't anymore."

17

"Ah," Tom pushed his glassed up with his middle finger and scrunched up his nose, a tick I'd noticed at dinner, "Your ex? The one in the band?"

"Magnus," I nodded, "It certainly didn't help having dick face go banging on about him, not that I'm still hung up on him, or that I hate him. It ended on…well… horrible terms. But we were civil, it was just the worst day to have it dragged up I suppose."

"What happened?" Tom raised an eyebrow, but then immediately frowned and shook his head. I noticed he swayed a little where he sat. Perhaps from a little too much wine. "Sorry, that's none of my business, you don't have to tell me."

But I was going to. I'd opened a floodgate. A stranger had offered an ear and I was going to use it.

"I can't have children," I blurted it out so fast, I wasn't sure it was even coherent, "Well, I haven't been able to have any. When I was seventeen they…the doctors found a cyst on my left ovary, it ruptured, and they had to remove the whole ovary. I was diagnosed with PCOS. The chance of me having children without medical intervention is… well… I don't know if there's a percentage, but I was told it was unlikely to happen."

"Shit…" the word fell from Tom's lips, but his eyes were fixed intently on me, not allowing me to look away and to continue my story.

"Mags and I met when I was twenty-one. He had this awesome, crazy life, he toured with his band. I was doing work experience at a recording studio. It started really casual, we were more mates than anything. He was great, Dena loved him too."

"He knew about my…problem," I stopped, another mouthful of wine, a bigger gulp this time, "I stopped deejaying when I was twenty-four, started focusing more on the production side of things and I told him I wanted a baby. We started trying straight away. It didn't happen. The abridged version... we had three rounds of IVF, I refused to try a forth time, and he told me if I didn't try again, he couldn't be with me any longer."

Tom was speechless. About as speechless as I had been when Mags had said those words to me just over twelve months ago. His mouth opened and closed a couple of times, as if he was try-ing to find some words which would be an appropriate response for what I'd just revealed to him. But he came up with nothing.

"He said he loved me, but he wanted a family, and if I wasn't willing to keep trying...then I obviously didn't want it as much as him."

"Ada, you know...I know that's not true. I don't know you, but I know that's not why you didn't want to try again," Tom's voice came out like he was trying to persuade me to believe him. To believe what I already knew.

"I know. He just didn't understand. It's my body. It was me going through the procedures and it was breaking me...I realised he didn't love me enough to accept just me. He'd always want a family and he'd always resent me for not being able to give him one," I sighed, "I'm sorry Tom, you don't want to hear all this. You must be so excited with you baby due any day, your lovely girlfriend. Grace is wonderful. You don't want me bringing you down."

"Appearances can be deceiving," Tom almost snatched the wine glass from me this time and took a big gulp. "You shouldn't as-sume someone has a perfect, happy life, just because that's the way it looks to everyone on the outside."

"What do you mean, how can you not be happy?" I wanted to

scream, but I managed to keep my voice level. I'd just told him everything I'd been through to have a child of my own. How I'd lost the one person who meant the world to me because I couldn't give him what he wanted, and he was sitting there telling me he wasn't happy? He wasn't happy with his perfect girlfriend and the new family he was about to have.

"It's not my baby," His words stunned me into silence. "My abridged version. We were together for two years, then we broke up for a while. Then we got back together everything was great, until she found out she was pregnant, and she was almost twelve weeks already. We knew from the dates it couldn't be mine, but everything was so perfect between us. She said she didn't want to risk losing me. She was going to get an abortion," I winced as he said the word. I understood people had their reasons and I wasn't anti-termination, but the thought of it still upset me. "I wouldn't let her. I didn't want to lose her, but I knew if she got rid of the baby she would end up hating me. So... I stepped up."

"Does anyone know?" Tom's story had shaken me. What a burden they both had to bare.

"Our parents, that's it," Tom nodded, passing the now empty wine glass from hand to hand. I picked up the bottle and poured the remaining wine into the glass. "It's been really hard, and I wasn't sure why I expected it to be anything else. I do love her."

"But?"

"But I know we're on borrowed time. She's not happy, and I don't think I can make her happy. I don't know what's going on in her head. She won't tell me," Tom let out a long defeated breath, "Intimacy has been non-existent."

"She is heavily pregnant," I found myself defending his girlfriend.

"We've had sex once since she found out and that…was awful. It was difficult, and awkward and not great for either of us. I've tried since, and I know it's not the be all and end all, but sometimes I think if she'd just let me show her how much I love her, she might realise. She might let me in. It's not just the sex though, she won't let me hold her, even kissing…well I try," I remembered the little peck he placed by her mouth at dinner. But when I thought back, he was right. He'd been attentive, pulling out her chair, helping her sit down, but he'd not touched her, there had been a clear void between them.

"It might be different when the baby arrives," I offered. But what did I know? "Once that tiny little baby is there, nothing else will matter, you obviously think you'll be able to love it as your own."

"Of course I would," He was a better man than most, there wasn't a hint of doubt in his words.

"I'm so sorry Tom, I was wrong to judge," guilt gnawed its way into my consciousness. But he simply shrugged. "Where is she now? We've been out here a while."

"Asleep, she went up a while ago, she gets tired," Tom explained, "She insisted I stay and enjoy the rest of the night."

"Well then you should."

"I am, believe it or not. Sometimes it's nice to talk to a stranger, get stuff off your chest," I took the glass off of him.

"Drown your sorrows," I raised the glass before taking sip.

"Enjoy the beautiful view," but his eyes hadn't left mine and I quickly caught on that he was not talking about the lake rippling under the pretty lights.

"Charmer," I laughed and tore my eyes from his suddenly intense azure gaze. My face felt suddenly very hot.

A few beats of silence passed between us.

"She told me I could sleep with someone else. That she wouldn't mind or blame me if I went elsewhere. With most women I'd think that was a test, but Grace is too serious for that," and that's when realisation struck me square in the face.

"Is that what this is?" I started, not looking at him, but out at the lake. "Are you propositioning me Tom?"

Tom took a very audible long shaky breath and exhaled loudly. I watched him from the corner of my eye, he sat staring across the lake, arms resting on his knees and empty wine glass dangling between his fingertips. "I think I need another drink."

"You don't strike me as the type to hit on weird, tattooed, goth girls," it was a bit of an over exaggeration of my appearance. Slightly alternative with a fondness for odd hair colours and wearing a lot of black. But my appearance, although I was quite happy with it, was a far cry from his pretty, blonde girlfriend, with her slender (albeit heavily pregnant) frame. I was tall, for a girl and I was what I liked to call voluptuous. I didn't consider myself fat, but some would, and I could probably stand to lose a few pounds. Although earlier in the day I'd been quite enamoured by Tom, after meeting his girlfriend I was quite certain, taken or otherwise, I'd never be the type of women he'd find attractive. But that was fine, everyone had their types. Even those who said they didn't.

"You've already had to apologise for being too quick to judge once this evening, let's not go there again," Tom chuckled rue-fully, finally turning to look at me and he set the empty glass on the step by his feet.

"I have a bottle of champagne on ice up in my room."

"Oh yeah, what's the occasion?"

"Came with the room, it's supposed to be for the newlyweds. Dena's guilt gift for not having me as bridesmaid," I half laughed.

"Well I can't let you drink that all by yourself, it would be ir-responsible of me," Tom leaned in, close enough for me to feel his warm breath on my lips. But only for a moment, because I pulled back, aware we would be in plain slight should any strag-gling guests wander outside. "You're beautiful Ada."

"I know."

"You shouldn't be so modest," his tone was sarcastic. So, I pushed myself up and wobbled slightly on my wine addled legs. I brushed the front of my knee length satin swing dress and looked down at him.

"Are you coming then?"

"Lead the way."

CHAPTER THREE

...Is a problem halved

Tom hung his jacket over the back of the dresser chair, whilst I went to pour the champagne. Although I knew the score, I knew neither of us had any interest in drinking it. The ice had completely melted, but the bottle still felt relatively cold. I wondered how much fizz would be left.

I felt the heat of Tom's body milliseconds before he pressed up against my back, and his hot breath was on my neck. A large hand rested just where my waist curved out to my hip. Tom was patient and he watched over my shoulder as I carefully poured two flutes. I was pleased to see a steady stream of bubbles racing to the surface of each glass. I turned in Tom's hold, separating us ever so slightly so I could put a drink in his hand.

"Are we toasting?" his voice was a low grumble.

"Should we be?"

"It's champagne..."

"Fine...to sob stories and sex with strangers."

"I'll drink to that," Tom agreed with a chuckle and clinked the rim of his glass against mine. When he took a sip, I noticed his hand was shaking and it occurred to me, through my tipsy haze that he might be nervous. I didn't have much time to contemplate that thought though, as I'd barely brought the glass away from my mouth, when I felt it taken from my hand. Tom placed both glasses on the table, and with no further preamble he brought his hand to the back of my neck and ducked his head, crashing his mouth to mine.

It was scorching from the offset. Tom didn't mess about, holding my face to his, he forced his tongue between my lips and met mine in a battle of wills. It had been a long time since a man had been so assertive with me, and to be honest I'd not expected it from him. Especially having seen his hands shaking just seconds before. My natural reaction was to give as good as I got. So caught up as I was in the kiss, I hadn't felt Tom's hand reaching for the zip on the back of my dress, until it was half way down my back.

Tom was the one to pull away first, but only move the fabric from my shoulders and let the dress drop to my waist. "Fuck." was the only word he uttered as my lace clad bust was revealed to him. I shimmied my dress over my hips and let it drop to the floor and slipped my shoes off, kicking them out of the way. Tom took a second, and the hungry appraisal his eyes gave my body was enough to make me painfully aware of the sudden throbbing heat between my thighs. I was sure I could feel my arousal dripping from me and soaking the crotch of my high waisted satin and lace briefs. I'd always been a believer in comfort coming first, particularly when it came to underwear. I'd long learnt that comfort didn't have to mean unsexy. Tom certainly seemed to approve.

I didn't let him dither. My hands were quickly on the buttons of his shirt. As I tried to make quick work of getting him out of the offending article, Tom's mouth dropped to my neck, and it was almost hard to focus on the task at hand. His series of nips and licks moved up and along my jaw, back to my mouth, "Bed," I mumbled against his lips. Tom nodded, and I pulled out of his grasp, and practically bounded across the room and threw myself onto the bed. I crawled round on all fours to see Tom chuckling as his shrugged his shirt to the floor and kicked his shoes off. He was working on his belt when he approached the bed and I crawled to the edge to meet him. I knelt back on my haunches and batted his hands out of the way.

I could feel Tom studying me, whilst I removed his belt probably slower than necessary. I was enjoying his interest in my body and it had been so long since I'd felt desired that I was purposely drawing it out. I unfastened his suit trousers and pushed them over his hips. I bit back a gasp at his now, very obvious arousal straining against his black boxer shorts. I leant forward, the desire to press my mouth against his fabric covered erection taking over.

I parted my lips and pressed them to the hard outline of Tom's erection, letting out a warm breath. "Oh, fucking hell, Ada," I brought my lips back together in a smirk at Tom's husky exclamation. I placed light kisses up to the waistband of his underwear and pulled back and peered up at the man in front of me. Tom's eyes were closed, and his head tipped slightly back.

I took that moment to admire his body for the first time. Clothed I took Tom to be skinny, or perhaps slight was a better description, despite his towering height, he was not a big man. But I was surprised, pleasantly so by the solidness of his torso. I'd expected a sharpness to his body, that comes with men who are a bit too thin. Ribs slightly visible, and that dip in the middle of the chest. But Tom's wasn't anything like that. Instead there was a layer of defined muscle under his flesh and a firm chest, emphasized by strong collarbones. Running my eyes downwards, he had one of those vee's, with a trail of fair downy hair disappearing into his boxers, and past that impressive bulge were two lean, well-muscled legs which went on forever. This was clearly a man who looked after himself.

But he was a far cry from what I was used to. My mind momentarily flipped back, and I couldn't help but remember Magnus' giant frame. Big, tall, broad, all hard and soft at the same time. I'm a sturdy girl, and far from petite. My ex-boyfriends larger than average frame had made me feel small in comparison. Safe.

Tom wasn't here to make me feel safe though, and I wasn't complaining. He had a great body. "Get back on the bed, Ada," I brought my gaze back up to see Tom now staring down at me. His pupils were blown wide, none of that cerulean blue visible, making them appear black in the dim light of the hotel room. The hunger in which he stared at me, and the assertiveness in his tone, caused me to obey his instruction without hesitation, and I fell backwards, untucking my legs from beneath me and shuffling up the mattress.

I gasped. Actually gasped, with the suddenness of Tom's attack. His body caged mine before I even felt him get on the bed and his mouth was on my neck, one hand tangled into my hair, pulling it, not to hard, but hard enough to keep me compliant. The other hand had sought purchase under my right knee, pulling my leg up to hook around his narrow waist.

I wanted to do something. Anything. But the complete domination of his position over me, rendered me motionless. I wasn't restrained, not really. I was free to move my legs and my arms lay idle at my sides. Eventually, realising if I didn't do something I was nothing more than a ragdoll beneath him, I moved my hands to wrap around his back, fingertips pressing into his flesh as his kisses turned into nips, and moved lower. His hand left my hair as he sunk down my body, his lips taking in the swell of my breasts. Sucking and biting. It was all I could do to just move a hand into his curls and encourage his worship of my body.

My nipples hardened and rubbed somewhat uncomfortably against the lace of my bra, and Tom's mouth sought them out. He bit, hard enough to hurt, but the pain was blunted by the fabric covering them. "These are spectacular my darling, this needs to come off," I hadn't been expecting his voice, and I must have jumped, as he sat up. My leg fell from its place on his hip and he straddled my thighs. Then he took my wrists and pulled me up. Tom looked into my eyes for a moment and offered a reassuring smile. I reached behind and unhooked my bra. He used both hands to ease the straps down my shoulders and remove it gently, letting my heavy breasts fall free of their confines.

Until that point Tom had been nothing but a gentleman. But the carnal urge of a man who'd been deprived of intimate female company for far too long took over in that moment. His eyes fixed on my chest, and I was sure he might have growled. At least a low grumble left his throat, before I was on my back again and his mouth was on my exposed breasts. A hand groped at one, large as his hands were, he struggled to grasp it entirely as his fingers plucked at my nipple, whilst his mouth worked on the other side, licking, biting, tugging.

I was not shy when it came to sex, despite my limited number of sexual partners, Mags and I had been rather deviant in our bedroom antics. I liked it rough, I liked to submit somewhat, although I'd never fully explored the extent of that kink.

But Tom wasn't dominating me in the traditional sexual sense of the word. He was not restraining me or spanking me or doing any real kind of fifty-shades shit. I had complete freedom to take control of the situation at any time I wanted. But I didn't want to. His entire demeanour showed authority over what was happening between us, and for some reason I just trusted him. I trusted this complete stranger not to hurt me, to look after me, and to ensure my pleasure. That comprehension turned me on more in that moment, than the things he was doing to my breasts with his mouth. "T...To...mm."

He didn't stop his ministrations which had travelled down to my abdomen, suckling on my soft flesh just below my belly-button. His fingers were now hooked over the elastic of my knickers. He spoke into my skin, "Yes, my love?"

'My love' seemed such an affectionate term to use, but one which gave me a warm fuzzy feeling inside. "Can I... fuck..." I couldn't form a coherent sentence as his tongue ran up my lace covered slit, and his warm breath sent bolts of pleasure shooting through my nether regions.

"You're positively soaked my dear, I can taste you through your knickers, shall we get them off?" I could only nod, and he finally dragged them down my legs. He didn't leave anything to me, as he unhooked them from my ankles and dropped them on the floor next to the bed, "That's better, now what did you want to do?" He hadn't dismissed my attempt to recover some control.

But I suddenly realised I didn't want it. I didn't want him to ask me what I wanted to do. I wanted him to tell me what I wanted.

I must have looked a little wide eyed and panicked, because he crawled back up the bed and pressed a calming kiss to my lips. He looked at me again, urging me to tell him, "Nothing... I mean... oh Christ...I want you to...can you tell me what you want me to do?" The words suddenly left my mouth, and the grin which spread across Tom's lips told me it was exactly the right answer.

Without answering, Tom settled down on the bed next to me. He kissed me a little more, soft, gentle, reassuring pecks to my lips and face. A far cry from the urgent, rough kisses from not so long ago. He stopped, only to reach down and arch his hips so he could slip his boxer shorts off. He kicked them to the ground and my eyes fixed on his cock.

I hadn't seen many 'real life' penis', but Tom's was certainly one of the more attractive I'd had the pleasure of meeting. Dena had once jested that men's cocks quite often looked like their owners (a bit like some dogs did). I'd laughed along, but this was the first time I'd really got the joke. Tom's erection lay against his stomach, long (or tall depending on which way you looked at it), proud, almost regal, in the way it curved ever so slightly. Big, but not grotesquely so. It suited him. I couldn't stop the giggle that escaped my mouth.

"That's not the usual reaction I get."

"I'm sorry, it's not... I just remembered something that...never mind," I shook my head and reached down, wrapping my hand around his length.

"Careful now," Tom all but gasped, his hand gripping my wrist, stalling my strokes, "It's been a long six months, it could well go off if you keep that up."

I frowned, "I hardly touched you."

"Spread you legs for me sweetheart," another swift turnabout, I reluctantly let go of him, and settled back at his instruction. His hand didn't let go of my wrist as he moved my hand above my head, then he found my other arm, and did the same. "I want you to keep your arms up here, can you do that for me?"

I wondered if he was this domineering in all his sexual encounters? I had a hard time believing Grace, although I knew little of her, would be even slightly kinky. But I obeyed. I couldn't help it. I just kept doing everything this frustratingly polite man asked of me.

Tom moved down the bed, between my legs, tweaking each of my nipples on the journey down my body. His fingers danced from my cleavage and down the centre of my stomach. I was aware of him drawing patterns on my flesh and the realisation that he was tracing the lines of my tattoo caused a fresh flood of moisture to gather between my legs, "Shit...Tom."

Tom just chuckled. A low, breathy laugh. Then he dropped and using his fingers to separate my folds his mouth was on me. He lapped away, enthusiastically. He nibbled at my lower lips, and danced his tongue around my entrance, then his lips encased my little bundle of nerves, already swollen from anticipation, and sucked, hard. Hard enough to make me squeal, and fling one hand down, thread my fingers through his curls and pull.

"Ada!" Tom stopped dead, reprimanding me in his tone. But I could only let out a sob of frustration.

"Please don't stop."

"Hand."

"Please."

"Put your hand back above your head."

Reluctantly, I removed my fingers from his hair. Instead, I brought my hand back above my head and wrapped them around my other wrist, nails digging into my flesh. "Good girl."

His mouth returned to its previous ministrations, but this time his fingers were there too. He didn't ease me in gently either. Two fingers slipped into me, curling upwards and pressing hard, moving, searching for that one spot, all the while his tongue fluttering on my clit, leaving me squirming beneath him. I bucked my hips, and words were leaving my lips. I wasn't sure what words exactly, nonsensical pleas. I was begging, for what I wasn't quite sure. I was a little drunk, and orgasms were complicated things. They'd never happened every time for me. I didn't expect them to, and alcohol didn't help. But somehow, the man between my legs seemed to be working some kind of magic on me. My mind didn't wonder for long, as there was a warmth building in my core, and my back was arching. I shamelessly ground myself onto his face, as my orgasm washed over me. I don't know at which point my hands had scrunched the sheets up, but as I came down, I realised I had the fabric fisted up, and I opened my eyes, gazing up at the ceiling.

Lips on my neck, jaw and mouth. I could taste myself on him, and that's when I came around from my post-orgasm induced coma. "I really need to fuck you, Ada," I figured I could move my hands now, and took the opportunity to wrap an arm around his shoulders, enjoying the feeling of his body on top of mine. His narrow hips settled between my thighs and he rocked back and forth, his length gliding up and down my slick centre.

I nodded, using my other hand to reach up and sweep his mussed hair out of his face, then remove his glasses for him, seeing they were steaming up. I reached over and set them on the bedside table. "Can you still see me?"

"Mostly, you're a little fuzzy around the edges."

"Hmm, that might be the Champagne and Chablis."

"Might be."

"Fuck me, Tom."

"With pleasure."

He drew back and reached down to line himself up with my entrance. He eased in slower than I would have liked, although I knew he was taking it slowly, he didn't want it over too quickly.

Tom's strength surprised me, as he gripped me behind my knees and dragged my body down the bed without breaking contact. His first few thrusts were slow, and careful. "Alright?"

I nodded, too breathless to speak.

That seemed to be the only confirmation Tom needed that he was okay to pick up his pace. His grip on my thighs was so hard it bordered on painful as he started pounding into me. His angle ensured with each thrust he hit parts of me which were already overstimulated from my orgasm, causing bolts of pleasure to rage through me. My back arched off the bed and Tom yanked me harder into his hips.

I wasn't sure at what point I'd started vocalising my pleasure. I'd never been one for loudness in the bedroom. But I was suddenly aware of the high-pitched yelps escaping my lips with each impact of Tom's thrusts. My vocal enjoyment seemed to spur him on, as grunts started accompanying his movements, and his pace, if possible, sped up. Our passion carrying its self away with it, we reached a crescendo, and very suddenly, I wasn't aware of anything other than the explosion of warmth in the pit of my stomach and the blinding whiteness before my eyes.

I'm not sure if I'd dozed off, or if hardly any time had passed at all when I felt the movement of the bed, and I scrambled up into a sitting position to see Tom in all his naked glory gathering his clothes together. When he turned back to the bed, whilst pulling on his boxers and suit trousers, he offered a sheepish grin, noticing me watching him. "I can't stay-"

"I know," I cut him off. I tugged the sheets around me over my lap, covering at least a small amount of my modesty.

"You were wonderful, Ada...superb," I pursed my lips and giggled as his evaluation of our tryst.

"You know, you can use the shower before you go back," I nodded towards the bathroom.

Tom paused his dressing, and his eyes darted to the bathroom door and back to me, "Would that be alright?"

"Of course," I wasn't about to send him back to his girlfriend smelling of sex and sweat. With a grin and a nod, Tom picked up the rest of his outfit and disappeared into the ensuite.

When the door clicked shut, I collapsed back onto the bed, tugging the sheets up around me, with the biggest shit eating grin on my face. I hated to say it, but Dena had been right. I'd needed to get laid and Tom had scratched an itch I hadn't even realised was there. And boy had he been thorough.

When Tom emerged from the bathroom ten minutes later, dressed and looking immaculate again in his tailored suit, his hair still damp and curling a bit tighter, I was still curled up in the bed enjoying the post coital bliss.

"Thanks for that, Ada, I appreciate it," He approached the bed and perched next to me. I peered at him from the little nest I'd created in the sheets. I wondered if he meant the shower or the shag? I felt it better not to ask though.

"Will you tell her?"

"Yes of course. She's always been honest with me. She told me to do this. Well not specifically this, you...here...but yes. I'll always be honest with her," It was an odd situation to be party to. Nothing about what we'd just done would normally be considered as acceptable. I'd never condone cheating in any situation. But Grace had permitted him to seek pleasure in the arms of another. Pleasure she was for whatever reason unable to give him. He clearly loved her in some capacity, because what other reason would there be to stay? It wasn't his baby, she wouldn't sleep with him, and it sounded like communication was an issue. He still doted on her. But like any man, or human really, he had needs. Not just sexually, but he clearly craved intimacy on other levels. Why else would he open up to a virtual stranger about the problems in his relationship? "Can I ask you not to tell Claudine and Matt? They believe I'm about to become a father..."

"I won't say anything," I promised.

"Thank you."

"Don't mention it."

"Are you okay? I wish I didn't have to leave, you look so cosy in there," he gestured to my cocoon.

"I'm perfect Tom," I assured him. "Don't worry about me, we're good. I had a lot of fun, but I know you need to go back to Grace, I knew what I was getting myself into."

Tom smiled. A completely perfect, beautiful smile. Then he leant down and brushed his lips over mine. I kissed back, just for a moment. "It was lovely meeting you, Ada."

"You too Tom."

And then, he was gone.

CHAPTER FOUR

An unexpected turn of events

Eight Weeks Later...

"This is utterly ridiculous."

"We'll let the doctors be the judge of that."

"It's people like me who are a drain on the NHS, honestly I feel absolutely fine, I'll just get a taxi home."

"Ada, I'm afraid we have a duty of care, I cannot let you go home."

The lady paramedic was kind, and attentive, and doing her best not to lose her patience, whilst she took my blood pressure from the back seat of the ambulance. We were currently weaving through the busy London traffic. "I just need to ask a couple more questions, have you ever experienced an episode like this before?"

"No."

"Have you eaten anything today?"

"I had a black coffee and a chocolate digestive at about nine thirty this morning,"

"Okay, is there anyone you need to call, to let them know where you are?"

"No."

"Are you sure?"

"Yes, it's hardly worth bothering anyone, I'll be in and out before you know it," I rolled my eyes. I really didn't have the time to be spending an afternoon in A&E. I was working to a deadline, and thanks to my morning meeting in the city I'd already lost precious time.

I'd been disembarking an underground train at Stockwell, to get back onto the Victoria line when I'd been accosted by an overwhelming dizziness and my world went black.

I'd come too sometime later, Paramedics already in attendance, still on the Northbound platform, with a small crowd of onlookers and rail workers nearby. I'd felt sick upon waking up and had almost immediately dispelled the contents of my stomach into a conveniently waiting paper dish being held by the female paramedic. The woman with fiery red, fuzzy hair, which had been pushed back into a tight knot on the top of her head, held the sick tray, whilst she explained to me that I'd collapsed and had been unconscious for almost twenty minutes.

The sicky feeling abated rather quickly and was replaced by an anxiousness to get home. I was hot, and sticky and all I wanted was a decent shower, lunch, and to get back to work. But against my instance that I was feeling absolutely fine, I'd still been carted into the ambulance.

To make matters worse, given our location, I knew I'd be taken to a South London Hospital. The closest Accident and Emergency department being Kings College and that was over an hour commute from my new home near Edgeware. None of this was ideal.

The hospital agreed with the paramedics that a trip to A&E was quite necessary. When we arrived, against my insistence to walk, I was instructed quite forcefully to sit in the wheelchair provided by an on-hand porter. I was then wheeled straight past the waiting room into the ward where I was seen by a nurse to be checked on almost immediately.

"Wow, gold star service," I joked when the nurse stepped into my bay pulling a trolley behind her and drew the curtain around the bed.

"Black outs are taken very seriously, Miss. Bloom," she told me, as she pressed a few buttons on the device next to me, preparing to take my blood pressure yet again.

"It was just a dizzy spell."

"Nevertheless," she shook her head, "Just relax your arm," she jotted down some notes and I shook out my arm when she removed the sleeve. "We need to take some blood samples, and a urine sample, I'll escort you to the toilets in the moment. Also, we're going to send you down to x-ray, because that wrist looks quite swollen."

I'd not even noticed the throbbing in my left arm until she'd mentioned it. I looked down and my eyes widened in alarm at the nasty purple bruising in the crease where my arm joined my hand. *Ouch*.

"Sure," I nodded in agreement and defeat. I was once again putting work before my health, something I'd been doing quite a lot recently. I was exhausted and finally sitting down and having nothing to do but wait, was making me realise just how much I'd been over exerting myself.

"I'm afraid we'll have to keep you in at least until your bloods come back from the lab, and then the doctor will be in to see you," I let out an audible sigh. This was a bloody inconvenience.

Three vials of blood, a trip to the toilets and an hour wait in x-ray later, I was back on the little bed, in a small ward. There were three other beds all occupied with patients suffering various ailments. I could tell I would be here a while. The good news was, my wrist was not broken, just badly bruised.

I snagged my handbag off the chair by the bed and riffled through it for a bag of cookies from the Mark and Spencer's bakery which I'd picked up and never gotten around to eating earlier in the day.

I'd just shoved a now slightly stale triple chocolate chip cookie into my ravenous mouth, when a voice caught my attention. "I thought it was you," I'd have not thought anything of the words being directed at me at all, as I was far too hungry for distraction. But the voice was strangely familiar. I looked up to find a face I most certainly knew standing at the end of my bed, chart in hand and a friendly smile on his beautifully bearded face.

"Tom!" My exclamation came out muffled through a mouthful of cookie, and I threw a hand over my mouth to avoid showering him with crumbs.

He grinned, "I saw your name on the board, and I thought, well there can't be many Adelaide Bloom's."

"One of a kind," I agreed, flashing an over the top bright smile.

"What the hell are you doing here?" My heart raced a little, he wore the same kind quirked smile on his lips that he had the evening of our tryst. When he'd leant over and pecked me on the lips before leaving me alone, but well and truly satisfied.

"I work here, Ada," he gestured to his ID card swinging from the purple lanyard around his neck, clearly indicating he was Doctor Thomas Cambridge – Cardiology.

"This is A&E," I frowned, "You said you were a Cardiologist, actually it says so right there," I flailed my pointed finger accusingly at his identification card.

"Ah yes, pit fall of NHS cuts, all of us consultants with relevant experience have to do one shift down here a week. I spent a year of my training as part of the resus team. Today's my lucky day."

"What are the chances?" I curled my legs beneath me, and got comfortable on the bed, and held my paper bag of treats out to him, "Cookie?"

"Better not, I'm working, save me one?" he quirked an eyebrow.

I scrunched up my nose and looked in the bag. "I can't promise you anything, I'm pretty hungry," Tom laughed. "How are you anyway? How's Grace, the baby?"

"Yes, she had a little girl, about six weeks ago now, Elsie," He didn't quite look at me as he told me this news. Instead he moved to draw the curtains around my bay.

"Oh, that's great news! Please send her my love," my words were genuine. I had no ill feelings towards the woman, she'd been pleasant enough when we'd met. And Tom? Well I'd never had a one-night stand before, but there had been no awkwardness when he left. We both knew the deal, and now, talking like this.

It was almost like it had never happened, it was just like chatting to an old acquaintance. That was fine, I didn't mind that. We'd both gotten what we needed that night.

"I will do," Tom nodded, "But actually I need to speak with you, about why you're here."

"Oh?"

"Well I can't treat you. Obviously, because I know you. It's not strictly allowed, and it would be unprofessional of me to see to your medical needs given our...history," I nodded in understanding, "But that does mean you may have to wait quite some time to be seen by a doctor. I've already called down to see if anyone is available to see you from another department, but it's likely you'll have to wait until the end of my shift at eight o'clock and the next consultant will see to you."

"You're fucking joking?"

"In fairness Ada, your bloods will be another couple of hours, and we're likely to admit you for observation, at least for one night, given the circumstances of your visit."

"Honestly, Tom, I don't have time for this. I've got work to do, and I'm already behind on a deadline. I didn't even want to come in, the paramedics insisted, but I'm fine!" The exasperation in my voice was evident, "Can I just discharge myself? If something major comes up in my blood results, I'll come back?"

"I'm afraid I can't let you do that, Ada. You collapsed in the middle of London and were unconscious for over twenty minutes. You have no history of blackouts, so it's important we find out what caused it, and to make sure it doesn't happen again. You could have really hurt yourself." Tom gestured to my bruised arm.

"I told the Paramedics, and the nurses, and I'll tell you... this cookie is the second thing I've eaten today, I had a biscuit and a black coffee this morning. I'm working eighteen-hour days on my current contract, I've just moved to a new flat, and I'm also negotiating a major contract. I'm probably just burnt out, Dena told me I was going to make myself ill. I just need a proper meal and a good night's sleep." I sighed, and Tom pulled the chair next to the bed closer and sat down. He took my hand and squeezed it reassuringly.

"Would you like me to call Claudine? Or anyone, to let them know you're here? I can see you've declined contacting anyone. I know Claudine would come and wait with you."

"God no!" I hadn't meant to raise my voice, and Tom had let go of my hand quickly, "Sorry, I'm sorry," I apologised quickly, "It's just, this really isn't worth worrying anyone with. I already feel like I'm wasting everyone's time as it is."

"I really don't think Claudine would see it that way, what about family?" Tom's expression was pleading, and I knew I wasn't going to win any sort of argument. I was here for the long haul.

"God, not my Mum! That's worse than Dena, she will not be hearing about this at all. I'm lucky she let me move back out as it is," I shook my head, "So, would it make it quicker for me if you could treat me?"

"That's not an option, Ada," Tom stood up and shook his head.

"There must be something I can sign. There's no part of my medical history that I care about you knowing, you already know most of it anyway. Who're you going to tell? Dena, Matt? They know it all. There's nothing wrong with me, which my bloods will show you anyway..."

43

Tom cut me off. "Alright, Ada," His voice resigned, and he rolled his eyes, "If you're sure, I'll send the nurse in with the forms."

"I'm sure," I nodded, "Thank you Tom. Honestly, I'll be out of your hair before you know it."

He chuckled and nodded, "Speaking of hair, I notice you've changed yours."

I reached up and touched my finger tips to the neat updo I'd managed to tame my hair into, attempting to look presentable for my meeting. Although it didn't hide my recent colour change. The deep violet it had been at the wedding was now a layered effect of aquamarine and yellow. "Thought I'd brighten it up for summer."

"The joys of self-employment."

"You don't like it?"

"It looks great, Ada," Tom shook his head, and smiled as he went to leave, "I've really got to get on with my rounds, the nurse will be in with your forms. Bloods will be a while. I'll get the nurses to bring you something to eat."

"Cheers."

Tom hesitated a little, hand on the curtain ready to draw it back round. I smiled brightly at him. "It's nice to see you again, Ada."

"You too, Tom."

People watching was a favourite past time of mine. My job was quite solitary most of the time. Only about ten percent of it was spent in studios or meetings with clients. The other ninety percent I was at home, with my headphones on, alone, for hours at a time. So being out and surrounded by people was a bit of a treat. The time passed quicker than I was expecting it too as a got wrapped up in what was going on around me.

I'd seen Tom pass by the nurses station a few times. He'd always look over, smile or wave. It was good to see him looking so well, considering he had a newborn at home, likely keeping him up most nights. I thought he'd be sleep deprived and last time we'd been alone together he'd been quite glum. Not now though, now he looked full of the joys of spring and honestly pleased to see me. No awkwardness whatsoever.

More than two hours must have passed when I heard Tom's voice outside my ward, where I could just see the nurse's station. I looked up to see him holding a clipboard, and a deep frown was etched into his forehead. He was saying something to the person at the desk, who was just out of my sight. When he glanced over towards me and then back to the desk, I realised it must be my results. I strained to hear what was being said, his concerned expression giving me sudden cause to wonder if something actually was wrong with me.

"Sorry, Sue," I watched him hand the paperwork over the desk, "If you don't mind, please call down to the lab and just double check that these are the right results for Miss. Bloom. I want then to confirm there hasn't been a mix up."

"Of course, Doctor."

"Tell them it's urgent."

"Yes."

My stomach churned. Something was wrong. I was ill. I felt fine, except for the throbbing in my wrist and a slight residual dizziness from my fall. But clearly something unusual had appeared in my results. An anomaly serious enough for Tom to want to check they were the correct results.

I spent the next twenty minutes watching every move outside the ward. Tom reappeared, and I couldn't hear what was being said between him and the nurse the desk. However, a few moments later the person he'd been speaking to came into sight as she slipped from behind the desk and headed into my ward. In my direction. "Miss. Bloom."

"Yes," I acknowledged her, searching her face to see if her expression would give anything away. But she was smiling, and a bit too bubbly for my liking. I automatically assumed this was to buffer whatever she was about to tell me and did little to comfort my now anxious stomach.

"I've arranged a more comfortable room for you, with a little privacy so Doctor Cambridge can discuss the results of your blood tests," she gestured vaguely to the corridor. "Do you feel well enough to walk, or would you like me to fetch a wheelchair."

"I can walk," I twisted so I could swing my legs off the bed and slipped my flat ballet pumps back on. I was surprised when I stood, at the sudden rush of blood to my head, and I stumbled ever so slightly.

"Here, hold onto my arm," the nurse offered her elbow, and I took it without argument. Dread settled in my stomach.

"I'm really ill, aren't I? There's something terribly wrong with me."

"Try not to worry Miss. Bloom. Doctor Cambridge will discuss your results with you very shortly. He's just making a few phone calls and he'll be with you," the nurse opened a door to her left and turned on the light just inside.

It was a basic room, like the little bay I'd just left, but instead of curtains, was surrounded by solid walls, offering more privacy. I perched on the edge of the bed and put my bag down next to me. "My names Sue by the way, I'll be sitting in with Doctor Cambridge in a few moments, as your chaperone, as the paperwork states," I nodded dumbly. She was the nurse which had brought the forms to me, and explained due to mine and Tom's acquaintance, any patient doctor discussions would have to be witnessed by a third party, "I'm going to get another chair."

Oh god. Another chair. That meant they'd be sitting down. Only bad news was delivered sitting down. She reappeared moments later with a chair which she sat next to the existing, more comfortable one beside the bed.

"I'm sorry that took so long," my eyes shot up to Tom's voice as he entered the room, "How're you feeling, Ada?"

"Not at all worried by the fact you've stuck me in a little side room to deliver my results," I responded sarcastically.

"Ah," he nodded, "Okay..." he trailed off. He wasn't apologising or telling me not to worry. I noticed then he looked pale, and his hands were clenching onto the clipboard in his arms tightly, as if to stop them shaking. "Let's sit down," he gestured to the seat beside him for Sue, as he sat, "I'm sure Sue here has explained she'll be witnessing for us."

"Yup," I nodded, and Tom took a long shaky breath. "Oh god, I'm really sick... is it bad?" acid rose to my throat and my head was suddenly pounding.

"Right," I hated all his stunted words. He must have delivered bad news to hundreds of patients. I suddenly realised why him treating me was such a bad idea. "So, your results... your urine sample shows a mild UTI, nothing serious, no need for antibiotics. Plenty of fluids and it should clear up on its own. You may not have even noticed it," I shook my head, "Bloods...you're very anaemic, your iron levels are extremely low. It's surprising it's taken this long for you to experience any major symptoms."

"Right, that's bad?"

"It's treatable, it will take a while, but with iron tablets and a healthy diet you'll feel much better in a few weeks," Tom explained, offering a reassuring smile, and I let out an audible sigh of relief. "But... your bloods did show something else, Ada. We had to look what could have caused an Iron deficiency, you're a healthy young woman. Your hCG levels came back as high...very high. hCG, I'm sure you're well aware is the hormone which increases with pregnancy."

I couldn't talk. I just stared at him incredulously as he delivered the news which had clearly made him so nervous. But it wasn't sinking in. "Your hCG levels indicate that you are most certainly pregnant, Ada."

I tried to force something out of my mouth, some kind of acknowledgment of what he was telling me. But I wasn't sure what to say, what to ask. I didn't even realise I was staring down and my hands had come to rest on my belly. I eventually looked up and made eye contact with Tom. He was staring at me intensely.

Finally, a choked sob escaped my mouth, followed by my complete refusal to believe what I was being told. "I can't be... that's impossible."

"I've read your medical notes thoroughly, Ada. I know your history. Unlikely, is what you were told, not impossible," Tom clarified. "I know this is a lot to take in, are you sure you don't want me to call Claudine, or anyone else…"

"No!" I shot back quickly, "Listen, this can't be right, there must have been a mistake, my results must have got mixed up, or something," As I said it, I remembered Tom asking Sue to double check with the lab. He'd thought the same as me when he'd first seen my blood tests.

"There hasn't been a mistake, Ada. I did ask the labs to double check. We also dipped your urine to be sure," Tom's eyes implored mine, and I knew there was only one question he wanted to ask. The one question he couldn't. Fortunately, good old Sue stepped in.

"Do you have a partner you'd like us to call?" I couldn't help but laugh, a soft chuckle leaving my lips.

"No, there's no one," but I didn't stop staring at Tom, just hoping he'd read what I was somehow trying to convey by eye contact alone. There was no one. There had been no one. Not before him, or after him. Since Magnus, he was the only man I'd slept with, just once.

"Would you like a cup of tea?" Sue finally asked, and I just nodded.

"I've called up to Early Pregnancy and arranged an emergency scan. They will check everything's healthy and establish dates. Sue will escort you up there once you've had your drink," Tom was in full doctor mode now, "I'm happy to discharge you. I've written out a prescription for Iron supplement and folic acid," he took a green slip from his clipboard and held it out to me. "Once you've had the scan they will offer advise regarding the pregnancy, but as far as the anaemia. You need to take it easy, plenty of iron rich foods. Try to maintain a healthy diet, which you should be doing with pregnancy anyway. Make sure you're getting plenty of sleep. If you have any concerns, please make an appointment with your GP. Have you registered with a local one yet?"

"Not yet," I mumbled.

"I suggest you make that a priority."

"Of course."

Tom nodded slowly, "Best of luck, Ada," he and Sue both stood at this point.

"I'll be back with your tea in a moment," Sue very quickly shuffled out of the room, and Tom went to make a hasty exit.

"Tom…"

"Ada," He shook his head slightly, and his eyes begged me not to continue.

"She's gone," I was referring to Sue, Tom nodded and closed the door ever so slightly.

"Not here."

So instead I slipped my phone out of my pocket and unlocked it and held it out to him. Silently asking him to put his number into it.

"I could lose my job," but he took the phone and put his digits in. I took it when he handed it back and quickly saved it.

"Thank you."

CHAPTER FIVE

I care about you

I stood in my kitchenette, slice of pizza in one hand and the grainy black and white image in the other.
Nine weeks and four days.

It looked just like a little disjointed kidney bean. The sonographer had pointed out the little flickering white dot which was my baby's heartbeat and declared everything looked healthy and just as it should. They took measurements and booked me an appointment at my local hospital for my twelve-week scan, and then I saw a midwife and spent an hour discussing my medical history and being asked every question under the sun, until I was sent away with a big card folder, declaring me officially pregnant.

I was going to be a Mum. It was all I'd ever wanted.

It was all I'd ever wanted when I was in a loving and stable relationship. If you could call what Magnus and I had stable? Our relationship had been based entirely on music and touring Europe, sometimes further afield. It was all late nights, drinking and parties. I'd always known a baby would be a huge lifestyle change.

But now I had the one thing I'd spent years wanting and I couldn't quite believe it. I'd given up hope of ever becoming a parent a very long time ago. It wasn't the right time, I'd just signed a twelve-month contract with a major recording studio. I lived in a one bedroom flat in which I could barely swing a cat, let alone a baby and the rent was already bleeding me dry.

But this was real, and it was happening, and despite the circumstances joy bubbled in my chest. I was pregnant, and I was going to be a Mum.

I fixed the picture to my fridge with an Eiffel Tower fridge magnet and grinned, before heading over to the other side of my open plan living area and turning on my laptop. I swiped my wireless headphones off my desk and put them round my neck and started turning on my gear. It had just gone half past nine, and I was still working to a deadline. A couple of hours wouldn't hurt.

I'd just grabbed another slice of pizza and was about to sit down when my entry phone buzzer went.

"The fuck?" I grumbled out loud through a mouthful of pizza. I picked up the dodgy old intercom phone, "Who is it?"

"It's Tom," my stomach dropped. What the hell was he doing here, and how the fuck did he get my address?

"Uh come in, first floor, second on the right," I realised in my haste to get home, and eat and work, I'd not messaged or called him. But I wasn't honestly sure what to say. There was so little I could ask of him. He had a life and a family.

I pulled open my front door, just as he was about to knock, and beckoned him inside by waving my slice of pizza. "I erm… wasn't expecting you."

"I should have called, but...well to be honest I thought you might tell me to fuck off after how I've behaved, and I'm risking my job taking your phone number, so I figured going the whole hog and getting your address wouldn't make much difference," he explained. There was a beat of silence and we looked at each other. He looked tired, and as shell shocked as I felt. But his eyes raked over me, and I suddenly felt quite exposed.

When I had got home, I was in such a hurry to tuck into my freshly collected pizza that I'd stripped out of my stuffy and uncomfortable but smart, meeting clothes and thrown on an old, ripped, and out of shape band tee shirt. Nothing else. Not even knickers. The t-shirt was big enough to cover everything, but I was very aware that one wrong move and Tom would be getting quite the view.

"So much for the healthy diet and rest," he gestured to the pizza and then to my headphones.

"I'm fucking starving, someone kept me cooped up in a hospital ward all day. I think the four hours lounging around on a hospital bed classifies as rest," I smirked, "Would you like a slice?"

"Erm, actually yes, if that's okay? I came straight from work, I've not eaten," Tom approached the open box and picked up a slice.

"Sit down," I told him, "Drink? I've got water, Pepsi, tea, coffee... beer which is unlikely to get drunk now."

"Ah, okay a beer. I think I need one," he nodded. I walked over to the fridge and fetched a bottle. "I'm not cross with you Tom. You behaved just as you should have. I should be apologising to you, for putting you in such a position. I guess it was my own stubbornness."

I plucked the scan picture from the front of the fridge and

walked back over. I took a seat on the little sofa next to Tom and set the beer down in front of him.

"Everything is okay then? With the baby?" he nodded to the picture in my hands.

"Yes. She said it's exactly what she'd expect to see at this stage, she estimated nine weeks and five days. There was a good strong heart beat..." I trailed off, "Would you like to see? I mean it doesn't look like much right now, but yeah," I offered the picture and he took it gently from my hands.

I let him study it in silence, waiting for him to work out exactly what he wanted to say to me. He set the picture down on the coffee table and turned to me, eyes searching mine for a moment as I looked at him expectantly. "Oh Ada..."

And to my surprise, I was pulled into his arms, almost onto his lap as he held me fast in a bone crushing hug. My entire body tensed for a few seconds before I relaxed and wrapped my arms around his back and buried my face in his shoulder. The tears had come from no where and now they were soaking his light blue shirt, staining it darker.

I was not a sensitive person, I liked to put on a hard front. But this was the second time Tom had caught me at my most vulnerable, and I wasn't sure what it was about him that made me completely trust him with my emotions. "I know, Ada, I can't even imagine how you must be feeling sweetheart."

"S...sorry," I mumbled into his shoulder, then forced myself to pull away. He didn't let me go. "God, I've ruined your shirt, I've got mascara and eyeliner all over it," my fingers touched the damp fabric, and the black smears now adorning it.

"Are you happy, Ada? I know you're shocked, but please tell me you're happy," Tom ignored my concerns about his shirt. He brought a hand to my face and cupped my cheek in his palm, stroking my tears away with his thumb.

When I smiled, he smiled to and I nodded. "I am happy."

"I know this isn't how you imagined it would be. But I am happy for you. I've got no intention of taking your happiness away from you and I'm so glad that I could be part of making this... miracle happen," his hand dropped from my face to my hand, "But I can't be a Father to your baby, Ada."

"I know," My acceptance took him by surprise.

"You... know?"

"I understand, you've got Grace and Elsie, I'm not about to go ruining that for you. I'm alright with it. I don't expect anything from you. You won't have trouble from me, I assure you," The disbelief he was feeling was evident in his facial expression. His lips parted and his brow furrowed.

"Well, I do want to help. I want to support you financially. I don't want my child to ever have to go without, or you for that matter. You're important to me. I can promise you'll be well looked after," he squeezed my hand and I looked down, watching his thumb rub circles over the cherry blossom which decorated my flesh down to my knuckles.

"I don't need your money Tom. Really... I'm going to be fine," but he shook his head.

"Let me do this Ada, we can do it through my solicitor if you'd prefer, but I'd rather just come to an arrangement between the two of us, if that's okay?" bloody hell, even whilst telling me he wanted nothing to do with me and my bastard child he was being a charming gentleman about it. At my hesitation to accept what he was offering, he threaded his fingers through mine and drew my hand to his mouth, brushing his lips over my knuckles. "I do care Ada."

"You don't really know me though?" I creased my brow, unsure how he could make such a statement about caring for me, or my unborn child.

"I know you're a good woman. I know you're strong and independent. I know you'll be a wonderful mother," his eyes darted from my face to my stomach and if I wasn't mistaken his eyes were glassy, like he was holding back unshed tears.

"What about Dena and Matt?" I'd not really thought about it until now. Although I'd known Matt almost seven years, and I'd not crossed paths with Tom until the wedding. But he was still their friend. Dena was going to ask me who the father was. I wasn't about to lie to them.

"I'd prefer it if they didn't know about me being the father, at least not yet."

"I can't lie to her!"

"I know what I'm asking of you, but if Grace found out she-" he stopped himself, and I watched him mentally calm himself, taking a few breaths, "Now really isn't a good time, just give it a few months."

"Months? Tom I've got under seven months. Please don't talk to me about whether this is a good time or not. I've just signed a twelve-month contract for work!" I yanked my hand out of his, "Why are you even here? If you're so concerned about Grace's feelings? You should be with her, she's probably wondering where you are."

"She's not at home, she's staying with her Mum for a couple of weeks she...she's not well," Tom shook his head, clearly not wanting to share this piece of information with me, "She's not coping well, she hasn't quite...taken to motherhood. She knows about us, about what happened, and I'm already blaming myself enough about her current mental state without adding this to it."

"I...I'm sorry, I didn't know," now I felt bad and I realised I had to be grateful that he'd made the effort to see me. He could have completely ignored me, he should have done. He and Grace were clearly going through a very difficult time, and he had a great deal of stress without another baby on the way by a different woman.

"I don't want to argue with you. Not now, not ever," I looked into my lap and nodded.

"I won't tell Dena."

"Thank you," Tom picked up his beer for the first time and took a swig. He released a long breath, and his shoulders relaxed. What should I say? There were so many things I should say, but it didn't seem right. Because I still didn't regret sleeping with him. I could apologise for not insisting he wear a condom. But that wasn't solely my responsibility and it was a bit late for that now anyway. I awkwardly tugged my oversized tee shirt to my knees and squirmed in my seat, feeling a bit awkward in the silence. I jumped when Tom spoke again, "Please take care, Ada, and contact me if you need anything," he set the beer down half drunk. "I'd like your bank details so I can set up some support. To help you with anything you might need before the baby arrives."

"Erm...okay..." I knew arguing would be futile. He'd made up his mind and at this point my refusal of anything he offered would cause him more distress. He was doing his best to do the right thing. By Grace, by me, and by our baby.

CHAPTER SIX

Surprise!!!

Twelve Weeks and three days.

The Singing Teapot was mine and Dena's favourite spot for decent coffee and the most indulgent homemade cake. We'd happened upon it about three years ago when Matt and Dena were house hunting in the Primrose Hill area of North West London. I'd been dragged along because apparently my opinion was just as important as theirs. Even though I wasn't the one buying or living in the house.

Ever since its discovery, Dena and I made regular visits to our favourite teashop. It was a quirky little place, which doubled up as a second-hand bookshop. It was owned by an out there young woman called Carmen, who lived in the flat upstairs with her husband and five year old son. We'd become close with the baker, always on hand to play guinea pigs to her new recipes and I'd even done the odd shift to help her out on busy days.

We'd not been for a while though, with the wedding, and my recent move. I'd decided it was the perfect spot to break the news of my pregnancy to my best friend.

I'd waited until I'd had my twelve-week scan. Partially, because

I wanted to get through the first trimester before telling anyone. But also, because even now, after seeing my little miracle on screen for the second time, seeing it wiggle about, and its little heart flutter away and being assured that everything was *absolutely fine,* I still didn't *feel* pregnant. Then there was the anxiety about Dena's reaction to the news and all the questions which I knew would come with it. How would my best friend come to terms with it when I could barely believe it myself?

I wasn't really concerned about Dena asking who the Dad was. I think that would be the least of her concerns. And bless her, she could be a little dim at times, and maths certainly wasn't her strong point. It likely wouldn't even cross her mind that I'd conceived on her wedding night. The news that I'd participated in a one-night stand however, would come as quite the surprise.

I'd already secured our favourite table in the far corner of the café and procured two of their Summer Special Strawberry Iced Teas, and two of the biggest chunks of White Chocolate Rocky Road from the counter (Eating for two and all). I saw Dena through the window and she waved excitedly.

"Oh yum!" my friend dropped her bag to the floor by the table and gave me a tight squeeze before taking her seat. She took a long drag of her iced tea through the straw before addressing me. "So, what's all this in aid of? If I didn't know any better I'd say you were trying to butter me up...or fatten me up."

"Well you know, we haven't done this in ages, and you're always working," I shrugged.

"I saw you Wednesday," she giggled picking a chunk of chocolate off the top of her Rocky Road.

"Yeah I know," I smirked at her.

"You're acting weird," She could see right through me. She always could. Dena slouched back in her chair and squinted at me, a frown forming on her brow.

"Don't frown, you'll make your wrinkles worse!" I teased her, and she stuck her tongue out.

"Spill bitch."

I stared at her hard for a moment, realising the only way to do this was to just say it. "I'm Pregnant."

Her expression remained blank for several seconds. Then she leant forward and shook her head a little. "That's not funny Ada, fuck I know we can both make some sick jokes sometimes, but that's below the belt, especially for you," She let out a harsh chuckle. She was right, between the two of us we could have quite bad taste when it came to our humour.

I reached for my purse which I'd left on the table and untucked the folded scan photo from the day before. I unfolded it and slid it across the table towards her.

"Fuck!" she only had to read my name in the top left-hand corner to know I was being deadly serious, "Ada!"

"Shush!" I hissed, not wanting to garner attention with her raised voice.

"This is... how?" she looked incredulous and couldn't take her eyes off the photo.

"Well...sex tends the be the usual way."

"Yeah but...you can't...I mean you were never able to...oh my god!" when she looked at me she was smiling. A big, happy, genuine smile.

"Unlikely, not impossible," I echoed Tom's words.

"Ada," She shook her head again, before leaving her seat and coming around the table to wrap me in her arms, "Oh god I'm so happy for you, I can't believe it! I'm going to be an Auntie!"

When she finally let me go and settled back into her seat. She was still bounding with excitement. "So how far gone are you?"

"Just over twelve weeks."

"How long have you known?"

"A couple of weeks, I was almost ten weeks."

"You mean you've known for over two weeks and you didn't tell me?" She looked affronted by this revelation. "What did your mum say?"

"Nothing yet, I haven't told her," I shrugged, "You're the first person I've told," Except for Tom.

"You mean you've been keeping this all to yourself? Babes why?" Dena had these big, deep brown eyes, and she had that puppy dog pout down to a tee. Right now, she was giving me a 'Puss in Boots' stare. Doing her best to make me feel bad that I hadn't told her my news.

"I just needed a bit of time. It's a bit of a shock you know."

"I'll say," she nodded, seemingly understanding, "Oh my god, who's the dad?" The question I'd been dreading. The part I'd have to lie about.

"I erm...well I'm not proud of this but, I kind of had a one nighter. I didn't really know him..."

"Shit me, it wasn't Dave was it? At the wedding?"

"No," It was easier to deny falsehoods, than to outrightly lie.

"Thank god for that, he'd make a terrible father," she laughed, but looked genuinely relieved. "So...you're doing this alone?"

"Of course not! I've got you!" I told her, my voice sounding chirpier than I really felt. I lifted my drink to my mouth and grinned at her over the rim of the cup.

"Of course you do babes!"

"I'm seeing Mum and Dad at the weekend, I'll tell them then," I explained, putting my drink back down and turning my focus to the chuck of Rocky Road.

"Jo's gonna lose her shit," I nodded at her words. My Mum certainly was going to 'lose her shit'. "How do you think your Dad will be?"

"I dunno," I shrugged again, I seemed to be doing a lot of shrugging, but the truth was there were so many questions I didn't know the answer to right now. "Hopefully happy, they're both usually happy as long as I'm happy. And I am...over the moon," that was one way of putting it I suppose.

"You'll have to move again though, which is shit, your place is tiny," trust Dena to think practically. Almost three weeks and I'd given absolutely no thought to my current living situation and its poor suitability as a home for myself and a baby.

"I've got a while to think about it."

"Not that long, six months, Ada. You could live with us, we have room. You know you're always welcome."

"I know, but I couldn't intrude on you and Matt like that. It's different when its just me, for a couple of weeks," I thought back to the month I'd spent with them after Magnus and I had broken up. "But I can't move myself and a new born baby in, for an indeterminate amount of time."

"I wouldn't mind!" I knew she wouldn't.

"But Matt might, it's his house too," I chuckled, "Thanks for the offer, lovely. But I'm sure I'll be fine."

Dena was still holding the scan picture, she turned her attention back to it, stroking her thumb over the image. "I just can't believe it."

"I know,"

"Will you..." She trailed off, biting her lip like she was unsure if she should continue. I raised an eyebrow questioningly at her. She coughed before continuing, "Will you tell Magnus?"

"Um..." That was something I'd given a lot of thought to. I didn't see him regularly, but we still moved in the same circles. I was still set to produce the bands forthcoming album. We sometimes bumped into one another in mine and Dena's favourite pub on a Friday night. "Yeah, I'm going to see if he'll meet up. I don't want him to hear it from anyone else."

"You're too nice."

"There's no bad blood, he'd do the same for me."

"Would he?"

"Yeah well," I didn't really want to talk about Magnus, "I'll wait a couple of more weeks. I want all my family to know first."

Dena nodded, then put the scan photo on the table and slid it back to me. She tucked a strand of her dark, almost chocolate brown hair behind her ear, appearing deep in thought for a second. Then she looked at me, eyes wide with excitement, "Oh my god Ada! We have to go baby shopping!"

I managed to dissuade Dena from her shopping idea. I insisted it was too early and I wasn't ready to start shopping yet. But also spun a little line about being tired. I didn't tell her about my collapse on the London Underground, but I did explain my Anaemia diagnosis.

Tiredness wasn't a complete lie. Following my trip to the hospital, over the past few weeks the gravity of my condition really hit me. I wasn't sure what had kept me going prior to finding out about the baby. But ever since it was like all the symptoms had bombarded me at once. I was dizzy and sick, and so fucking exhausted all the time. I'd slept more than I'd done in years and I was having to make a real effort to eat properly as almost everything tasted funny and made me feel nauseous.

Dena had been understanding, and after another drink we'd parted ways. I'd be seeing her the next night anyway. We had two standing dates a week in which I went to hers and stayed over. I even had my own room in their house.

But in truth, shopping was a current bone of contention for me. The first payment from Tom had gone into my bank that morning, and I had no idea what to think about it, let alone what to do with it.

I'd heard nothing from him since the night he'd come to see me. Although I didn't expect to, he'd made it clear he would not be a father to the child. I didn't expect him to keep in touch with me. But yesterday morning a text arrived out of the blue.

Your twelve-week scan must be this week. How is everything? Tom

It took me by surprise and I wasn't sure how much I should tell him. Did he want to know how I was, or just that the baby was okay? Did he want to see the scan photo? I doubted it, he'd seen the first one, in which the baby resembled nothing more than a kidney bean. The most recent one, you could see the clearly formed head, body and limbs. The sonographer had told me that in as little as four weeks, they may even be able to determine the sex if I wanted to know.

In the end I kept it simple.

I had the scan yesterday. All is well, and as it should be. Ada x

I assumed he must have been working as it had gone lunch time when a reply came through.

I'm happy to hear all is well. And how about you? Are you okay? Tom

I tapped my reply quickly, deciding to once again keep it brief. In my mind it was best not to get attached. It was nice of him to check in, but it would be easier in the long run if we kept emotion out of it.

I've been very tired but feeling much better this week. Thank you. Ada x

When I checked my bank the next morning a deposit of five-hundred pounds had been made into my account by T A Cambridge. I felt physically sick, that was a lot of money.

What did he expect me to do with that sort of money? I was only twelve weeks pregnant, I didn't want to start shopping yet, it was still too early. But he obviously didn't think so. I knew preparing for the baby wouldn't be cheap, but I did have my own savings. I also knew my family would be eager to help me. There would be plenty of hand me downs from my brother's baby. I'd shot him a text to thank him.

Thank you. But it's far too much. Ada x

He responded almost instantly.

It isn't just for the baby, you'll need things too. It's for anything you need. Tom x

I'd not replied to that because I knew there would be no arguing. But the money still sat in my bank, untouched for almost a week before I put four-hundred pounds into my savings. Then went shopping and filled my cupboards with healthy foods and treated myself to a couple of new bras.

Because he was right, there certainly were things that I needed.

CHAPTER SEVEN

Well this is awkward...

Sixteen Weeks

It was another four, uneventful weeks of work and navigating a cacophony of odd pregnancy symptoms which I had no idea were even a thing, before I heard from Tom again. Once more it caught me completely off guard.

I'd been between a morning appointment with the midwife and a lunch meeting with an artist I was set to be working with in a few weeks. I barely had time to stop as I scanned my eyes over the message.

I need to speak with you. When would be a convenient time to call? Tom

How courteous of him, I thought, normally people just call. But I was glad he hadn't, because I was already running twenty minutes late and I didn't have any time to speak to stop and chat.

Sorry I'm just on my way to a lunch meeting and then I'm straight to the studio. I'll text you when I'm done. Ada x

I hoped it didn't sound too rude, and he simply text back

No Problem. Tom

The rest of the day passed in a blur of lunch, the underground and a non-airconditioned recording studio. The truth was, it was gone six o'clock and I'd just stepped onto the pavement outside Matt and Dena's closest underground station when I remembered Tom's text. It was Tuesday evening and I was on my way, having finally finished work to spend my usual dinner and girly veg out with my best friend.

I struggled to procure my phone from my pocket, whilst my arms were laden with various bags and I had my guitar on my back. I tapped a quick text to Tom.

Today has been crazy and I'm literally just going to Dena's. Can I call you tomorrow? Sorryyyy. Ada x

I hit send as I walked up the steps to the front door of Matt and Dena's four bed Hampstead townhouse. I shoved my phone back in my pocket and fished in my bag for my keys. Yes, I even had my own key.

Struggling through the front door, squeezing myself into the hallway, I called out, "It's meeee!"

There was no response for a moment, but then to my utter surprise and delight, with a jingling collar, and a tapping of paws on the hardwood flooring an adorable black dog rounded the corner. Matt and Dena didn't have a dog. At least they hadn't had one last Friday when I was last in their house.

"Oh, who are you? Aren't you lovely," I dropped to a crouch and fussed the dog's ears.

"Ada, can you still eat Curry?" Dena's voice boomed down the hall from the direction of the kitchen at the back of the house.

"Of course I can still eat Curry you bellend," I called back, with a laugh, then struggled back to standing, with the weight of the guitar on my back and beckoned the dog to follow me, "Hey Dena whose dog is this?"

"I'm sorry, he's mine," my heart dropped into my stomach. I knew that voice. I entered the open plan kitchen to find Dena mixing up a jug of Pimm's and Tom sitting at the breakfast bar, cradling what looked like a tumbler of whiskey, "Hey Buddy, come here," He patted his leg, and the obviously young dog, yipped and flew to his owner.

Tom locked eyes with me, looking quite sheepish. *So that's why he wanted to talk to me?*

"You remember Tom from the wedding, don't you?" Dena asked, as she pottered around the kitchen.

"Of course I do. Hi," I smiled brightly, suddenly quite proud of my ability to act on the spot as if I'd only met the man once.

"Hi, Ada," he nodded at me.

"I meant to text you, Tom's staying with us for a few weeks. Him and his ex-girlfriend have just sold their house, and his new place isn't going to be ready until next month. He was going to stay in hospital digs," Dena turned her nose up, as if the prospect of staying in Doctors accommodation was too awful to think about.

"I'd have been okay. But you know what Dena's like. She insisted," Tom rolled his eyes.

"You were going to put Buddy in a kennel!" Dena once again looked appalled, "I told Matt that he must insist that Tom stays here. Besides, you shouldn't be alone right now Tom." Dena gave his arm and affectionate rub, and Tom looked more than a little uncomfortable. "We fix broken hearts here don't we, Babe?"

She was addressing me, "She forced me to live here for almost a month when my ex and I broke up," I explained briefly. But suddenly so many things were whizzing through my mind. *Tom and his EX?* He and Grace had broken up? When? Clearly a while ago if the house had already sold. Although London property was prime and did snap up quickly. Why hadn't he told me?

"You're too kind Dena," Tom tilted his glass towards her, "Generous to a fault, Matt picked a good woman."

"Try telling him that," Dena scoffed.

"Uh oh, what's he done now? You've only been married two months," I couldn't help but laugh. Dena was always laying into Matt about something and bless him, he loved her and he just took it. But the phrase 'long suffering' came to mind. He got very little say in the dynamics of their life, but he seemed quite happy to let Dena steer the ship.

"Just being a typical ungrateful man about everything," she huffed, and I caught Tom shift awkwardly in his seat, and look down. A change of subject was in order.

"What's this about curry then?" I asked.

"I couldn't be bothered to cook and I thought as it's Tom's first night here we'd get a take away. It's nice weather, we can sit outside on the decking," Dena explained, just then Matt came into the room, and approached me immediately, taking the bags which for some reason I was still holding onto from by hands and setting them down, and then removing my guitar from my back.

"Ada, you need to be more careful, you shouldn't be carrying all this stuff," He gestured to the pile of crap I'd lugged along with me, which now sat on the floor. Then he enveloped me in his arms, "How did the appointment go, I bet Dena forgot to ask didn't she?"

"Actually," Dena burst in, "I'd not had time to ask yet, she literally just walked in, and I was telling her about Tom."

Tom and I shared a look, as the newlyweds carried on bickering for a few moments. When Matt released me from his hold, I took a few tentative steps to the breakfast bar and reached for the open bottle of lemonade, so I could pour myself a glass. "Sorry to hear about you and your ex," I told him quietly, not quite meeting his eyes.

"It wasn't wholly unexpected," His reply was just as quiet.

"Ada's pregnant!" Dena announced loudly to Tom, as if needing to explain Matt's treatment of me, unburdening my heavy load, and berating my best friend for not asking after me. I suddenly remembered that as far as they knew, Tom and I had only met the once and he had no idea I was with child (much less his).

"Oh well, congratulations," Tom smiled at me, "How far along are you?" He knew how far along I was.

"Just over sixteen weeks,"

"So how did it go with the midwife?" Dena finally asked, as she started riffling through a kitchen drawer, I presumed for a take away menu. I had to tell her, but I also didn't want to talk about it in front of Tom. I didn't want to rub it in his face. On top of all that, it made my lie feel so much worse. But how could I avoid discussing it? I watched Tom glance over at Dena, who wasn't currently looking at us, then he turned back and nodded at me, as if to let me know he was okay with me talking about it, and I self consciously ran a hand over my stomach.

"Er... yeah, well... she just checked my blood pressure and stuff, asked how I was... listened to the baby's heartbeat," I smiled at the memory.

"Really...you can hear it already?" Dena looked surprised and excited all at once. "Oh, I hope I'm not working for your next one so I can come, I think I'll cry!"

"I'd like that," I leant down to pet the dog which had come sniffing round at my feet once more.

"Buddy..." Tom's voice had a gentle but firm tone.

"Oh, it's okay, I adore dogs," I assured him, "And this one is absolutely gorgeous, Lab?"

"He is," Tom affirmed.

"How old?" I queried, happy to be on a more comfortable subject.

"Around six months," Tom answered.

"Oh, so you're still just a pup," I addressed the dog, who excitedly nuzzled my palm. I wanted to ask Tom a million questions. When had he and Grace broken up? What about the baby? Did Dena and Matt know he wasn't the real Dad? They'd not mentioned it, which made me think they probably didn't. It's not the sort of thing you openly talk about. Why on earth had Tom got a puppy when his girlfriend was pregnant? It doesn't seem like the ideal time to start adding pets the family.

"He was a bit of an accident really," Tom started, "We...me and my ex were visiting a family friend of hers who breeds Labradors. Buddy was the last one left in his litter, I fell in love. I couldn't leave without him."

"I can see why," I grinned up at Tom who'd answered my question without realising, "She was erm…pregnant, wasn't she? Your girlfriend?" *What the fuck was I doing?*

"Er yeah…" Tom nodded, but looked uncomfortable.

"Ada," I looked at Dena who shook her head, willing me to shut up.

"Oh, sorry Tom, I didn't mean…none of my business," I shook my head, and stood up straight, wincing as my back clicked. Damn ligaments.

"Don't worry, it's ah…" I'd put him on the spot, and I felt a bit guilty, "It's complicated."

"And none of my business," I gave him a hard look. One that screamed 'We will be talking about this later'. But we couldn't talk about anything now, not under Dena and Matt's roof. Fortunately, my rumbling stomach broke up the awkward quiet that followed. "So that take away?"

"I'll order it now," Dena nodded, "Usual?"

"Yup, I'm going to grab a shower and get comfy,"

*

"Ada…" I jumped when I walked out onto the decking, it was empty, save for Tom, who was setting the table ready for us to eat. I looked back through to the kitchen and couldn't see Dena.

"Where are Dena and Matt?" I wondered out loud.

"Matt's gone to collect the food, delivery was going to take ages, Dena's just getting changed," he explained.

"Okay," I nodded and pulled out a chair.

"I tried to warn you..."

"Not now, Tom."

"I'm sorry."

"I know, but we can't talk now."

"I just need you to know –"

"Oh, thank you, Tom you didn't have to do this," Dena swanned out on the decking, making us both jump.

"Least I could do." Tom told her dismissively.

"Oh Ada, look at you!" Dena was facing me now, taking in my new attire. I'd changed into some leggings and a comfy vest. It fitted me much closer than the stripy skater dress I'd been wearing when I arrived. I consciously rested my hands over my lower belly. I wasn't really showing yet, but I'd gained a bit of weight and there was an obvious bloat.

"I know, but I'm sure most of it's food at this point, I can't stop eating, yesterday I had two breakfasts –" She cut me off.

"I'm not talking about that, I'm talking about these," She launched forward, both of her hands covering my breasts and pushing them up, she laughed. I didn't, and I knew my reaction threw her, as I squealed loudly and stepped away, wrapping my arms around my chest. I wasn't body conscious. I had big boobs and I was proud of them. Dena and I had been in various states of undress together over the years, her grabbing my boobs was not unheard of.

"Do you mind?" I squeaked.

"Shit, sorry... do they hurt?" my face felt hot, and I knew it was because Tom was there, watching the scene unfold before him. "It's just, you've been wearing so many baggy clothes and they've got even bigger, I didn't think it was possible."

"You only saw me Friday. They aren't that big," I replied defensively, "I mean, big-ger."

"Are you kidding me? I can see you spilling out of your bra," Dena snorted.

"This is a new bra!" I cried through a laugh.

"I wish my boobs would get bigger," She pouted and looked down at her own small bust. She'd always envied me in that department.

"You really don't," I shook my head, but I almost choked on my laughter when I caught the way Tom was now looking at me. His eyes were drinking me in, roving up and down my body and lingering on my chest. He shifted when he realised I'd caught him and sat himself down at the table, quickly averting his gaze.

I tried to pay it no mind. He was a man and tits were mentioned. He as going to look, regardless of how inappropriate it might be that it was me.

Matt returned with the food and we all sat down to eat at the patio table. I was pleased because the attention turned away from me for a while. Matt and Tom were chatting between themselves, and Dena and started yapping away about some drama which had gone on in her office earlier in the day, something about her sexist, pig of a boss and the new secretary.

But I couldn't stop my eyes wandering over to Tom. The way he sat, listening avidly to his friend. I could have done much worse. He was smart, that was certain, being a doctor and all. He spoke well, he'd clearly come from good stock, but he seemed normal, whatever that was? He didn't act better than anyone else. He was good looking too, it went without saying. Finding out I was pregnant had knocked me for six and I'd not really looked at Tom properly since our one night together and now he appeared so much different to how I remembered. That day at the hospital and then in my flat, he'd been in his work clothes, smart grey trousers and a light blue shirt tucked in at the waste and rolled up to the elbows. He'd looked good sure, but now he wore faded black jeans which had seen better days, they fit closely to his perfect arse, and long, lean legs. The t-shirt he wore was grey, and old. I could tell it was old, because although it fit taught across his strong chest, there were frays around the neck and it was a bit baggy and out of shape around the bottom. He was in his comfies and damn did he wear them well?

"Ada...Ada, are you listening to me?" I felt like I was coming to. Dena's voice came into my consciousness, "Adelaide Bloom!" Her sudden shout of my full name snapped my attention solely onto her and I felt a little embarrassed as Tom and Matt both turned to look at me.

"S...sorry...I zoned out for a second. Baby brain, " I shook my head, but Tom arched an eyebrow. He knew I'd been looking at him. Thinking about him.

"Bloody hell," Dena shook her head and laughed, "I asked how your Mum is? Did you enjoy Brighton, I hope you relaxed?"

77

"Ugh! Mum's a pain the arse as usual and no, I did *not* relax," I was grateful that my embarrassing little moment had been swept over, but I did not relish the thought of talking about my delightful family either. Don't get me wrong, I loved them all to bits, but ever since finding out that I'm 'With Child' my Mother has been treating my like I'm made of glass. "She had me up at seven both mornings for...get this...*Pregnancy Yoga!*"

"Pahahaha!" Dena exploded laughing and even Matt chuckled and shook his head. "You? Doing Yoga?"

"Tell me about it. Then she kept making me these foul smoothies, and she had one of her crystal friends come to the house to cleanse my aura or some shit. I had to get Dad to sneak me a bottle of Pepsi in because I was craving fizz so much and I had a headache from hell because she wouldn't let me have anything with caffeine. She's a nightmare, Dena."

"At least your Dad understands," Dena said, sympathetically.

"I think Dad's in denial," I chuckled, shaking my head slightly, my poor Dad. The news of my pregnancy had thrown him for a loop and he'd not been quite sure what to say to me. He wasn't cross, or disappointed. It was just a reminder that his little girl was not so little anymore and he wasn't sure how to deal with that.

"She does have a point about the caffeine," Matt cut in, "You said you were going to cut down, but you haven't. You also drink more carbonated drinks than you do water. It's so bad for you."

"Alright, Doctor Tate." I scoffed at him.

"I am a Doctor, Ada. I know what I'm talking about. Back me up Tom," Matt nudged his friend who suddenly looked like a deer caught in the headlights. His mouth opened like he wanted to say something, but he knew he needed to consider he words wisely.

Fortunately for him, Tom didn't get chance to back Matt up, because I snapped far too quickly. My cutlery clattered onto my plate and tears clouded eyes in an instant. Stupid hormones. "I didn't come here to have you two gang up on me. This is my body and my baby, and I think I've already given up a hell of a lot in the last few weeks. I've just told you how I've spent my week-end off with my scatterbrain mother forcing her spiritual well-being mumbo jumbo on me. I don't need shit from you as well. You're supposed to be on *my* side!"

Dena opened her mouth to say something but closed it very quickly. Obviously rethinking whatever she was about to come out with. I should stop, I knew I should just shut up. But I'd been bottling for weeks. Trying to act how everyone assumed I should be acting – the glowing, overjoyed, mother to be. But the honest truth was that I was terrified. All I wanted to do was tell my best friend everything and I couldn't because I'd made a promise to Tom. Then seeing Tom, without warning, having him sit there and look at me, and hear all about my pregnancy, all the while acting like I was a perfect stranger to him.

A choked sob escaped my lips.

"I've had enough of being told what to do by everyone. You are all so worried about the baby and of course I don't want to do anything that's going to put it in danger. But what about me? No one has even asked how I am? Everyone is just assuming that I'm floating around happy as Larry because I'm not barren and I do actually have a functioning reproductive system. But there's a lot of things I don't have, I don't –" I stopped short. It was Tom that did it, he brought both hands up and rubbed his palms down his face, and his eyes were red. I was upsetting him.

I was upsetting him. It was almost laughable.

"Ada," Dena's voice was softer now and she reached over and rested her hand over mine. "I'm sorry."

"No, I'm sorry," I sniffed and rubbed my nose with my wrist, "Stupid hormones."

She laughed at that and when I looked over at Matt he looked stunned. I'd never lost my rag in front of him before and only a couple of times in front of Dena, naturally I'm pretty chilled out most of the time. They must all think I'm so ungrateful. They'd both been nothing but supportive since they were told the news.

"I'm going to get some drinks, anyone else?" Matt stood from the table, "Want to help me Tom?"

Tom nodded and stood from the table, giving me one last fleeting glance before he went inside, so Dena and I could be alone.

CHAPTER EIGHT

Conversations

& Explanations

Dena told me later that evening that she and Matt had been waiting for me to have some kind of melt down and she was quite relieved that it had finally happened. Even if at the dinner table with a guest wasn't the ideal time for it.

After we'd finished eating she'd taken me upstairs and we vegged out in the guest room, which had been my room in their house ever since they'd moved in. We put on Netflix and Dena painted my nails and pampered me until it was time to turn in for the night.

We both had a little cry and she hugged me and rubbed my barely there bump. We didn't see the men for the rest of the evening and I was thankful. I didn't think I could face Tom after my little episode. He likely thought my outburst was for his benefit and now considered me a mental, attention seeking, bitch. I knew I shouldn't care what he thought of me, but I did. Of course I cared.

I wasn't angry at Tom for not telling me about his situation with Grace, but I was confused. He'd asked me to lie to my best friend and I needed to know why? If he wasn't in a relationship with her or playing daddy to her illegitimate child, then why did he want nothing to do with mine? I needed answers and now after my dinner table melt down, I was quite worried that Tom would be less than willing to give them to me.

The house was quiet when I woke up the next morning. Matt and Dena set off to work early and my work day started whenever I wanted it to. However, I'd already decided after my busy day of meetings and time in the studio the previous day, that I'd take the day off. That plan was cemented when I woke up, eyes sore from crying and with a pounding headache.

I peered at my phone and the time read nine thirty-eight. There was a text from Dena, telling me she'd arranged to finish at lunchtime, so we could do something together and that she loved me. Another flood of guilt washed over me for my behaviour from the night before.

Then I remembered Tom.

I peered out the bedroom on the first floor. Across from my room was the second guest bedroom which Tom must be currently using. The third guest room is Matt's music room, come study. The opposite door was slightly ajar, so I tiptoed across the hall and peered through the gap. The bed was neatly made, and a pair of checked pyjama bottoms were folded neatly atop the pillow. I could tell the curtains were open from the light spilling into the room. I let out a sigh of relief, it appeared Tom had also gone to work for the day.

I took advantage of the shower in the guest bathroom. It was one of those luxury ones with jets in the walls with perfect adjustable water temperature. I always enjoyed showering at Dena's house, it was much better than my over bath shower head, which switched from hot to freezing and back again with no warning.

Feeling refreshed, I pulled on a little flared sundress in a pleasant peach shade and headed downstairs with my laptop under my arm. I heard a little jingle as I entered the kitchen and smiled to myself when I saw Buddy lounging on his doggy bed. His head had picked up when I'd entered the kitchen and now he was watching me curiously, head tilting side to side.

"Hello gorgeous boy," I greeted him. At my voice, he got up and came to sniff at my ankles, whilst I set my laptop up on the counter and then began fiddling with the coffee machine.

A short while later I was successfully pouring myself a large cup of black coffee, so strong I could probably stand my spoon up in it, whilst singing along to Lady Gaga (my happy music) and working out what I could make myself to eat.

I danced my way across the kitchen, narrowly avoiding the dog at my heels and opened the fridge. I'd just hit a particularly high note on 'Edge of Glory'.

"You have a fantastic voice."

The eggs I'd plucked from the top door shelf fell from my hands as I jumped violently at the interruption and grappled for the edge of the counter for support.

"Fuck!" I shouted, before spinning round to face Tom, and snapped accusingly, "Don't fucking do that!"

"I'm so sorry," he did look genuinely apologetic as he stepped inside the kitchen and reached out to me. I wasn't sure what he wanted to achieve by touching me, but I automatically jerked away.

"Don't creep up on people," I chastised him, hand going to my chest. My heart was still racing at the shock I'd just suffered.

"I really am sorry, Ada," he said again. Then he looked down and frowned, "Buddy, stop."

Buddy was lapping at the raw egg which now decorated the tiled kitchen floor. He looked up at his owner, before completely ignoring him and going back to his unexpected snack. "Buddy," Tom pointed at the dog bed. Buddy whined and skulked back to his bed.

"I thought you were at work," I stated, as I went to fetch a mop to clear up the remaining mess.

"No, I booked some emergency leave to get the house sorted. Stop doing that, Ada. Let me," He reached out to take the mop from me.

"I can manage."

I quickly cleaned up the mess then turned my attention to my coffee, and to Tom. It was then I realised his attire. Matching black Nike sports shorts and t-shirt. A pair of running shoes on his feet, and his phone clutched in his hand with earphone cables wrapped around it. It didn't take a genius to work out that he'd been running. Fuck, he looked good. His cheeks were rosy from exertion and his hair was damp with sweat and clung to his forehead. Just like his t-shirt clung to his clammy chest and stomach, showing off that defined muscle which I knew was underneath. I bit my lip to stop the whimper that was caught in my throat from escaping my lips. I blamed the hormones for the warmth which suddenly settled between my thighs.

"I'm glad I caught you alone, Ada. I'd like to explain everything...but first, are you alright? I feel awful about yesterday and I know you're fragile at the moment. My being here was a shock and I feel responsible for last night, and your... um... for what happened."

That pulled my thoughts out of the gutter. I looked at him, widening my eyes. Incredulous.

"My what, Tom? My outburst? Melt down? Don't flatter yourself, it was not for your benefit."

"For your distress, Ada. I feel responsible for causing you distress, because you weren't prepared for my being here," he shook his head.

"I should have called you when you text me," I admitted. That's why I wasn't cross with him. Because he had tried to tell me. It was never his intention for me to have to walk into the situation unprepared. "Why didn't you tell me about you and Grace?"

"Aside from the fact that it was none of your business?" I balked at that. Then as if realising what he'd said he shook his head. "I didn't mean it like that."

"You made it my business when you asked me to lie for you."

"It's complicated, Ada. I didn't tell you because I didn't want you to blame yourself."

"She left you because you cheated on her?"

"Partially. It certainly didn't help. I was honest with her, like I said I'd be. She didn't like it, but she accepted it. I assured her it didn't affect my feelings for her, and that I still wanted her and the baby. Then she went into labour, and everything changed," Tom took a few steps back and perched on the edge of the stool by the breakfast bar. "She refused to let me in the delivery room, she refused to see me for a long time after the birth. When she did see me…she wouldn't let me hold the baby. She wouldn't let anyone hold the baby."

"She left you?"

"Not immediately. We came home from hospital, and it was awful. The baby was screaming constantly, and she wouldn't let me or anyone else help her. Eventually her Mum turned up and Grace allowed her to help with the baby. But the baby was undernourished because she was struggling with feeding and refusing the help. She said it wasn't my fault, but she needed some space. She went back to America with her Mum and the baby, that was about eight weeks ago," Tom let out a long breath when he'd finished his explanation.

"So, you were still together when you found out about me?"

"Technically yes, a couple of days before she'd called me and asked me to put the house on the market. She didn't say as much but I knew it was over."

"I'm so sorry, Tom."

"It's not your fault. I told you before, we were on borrowed time."

"Do Dena and Matt know that it's not your baby?"

"Yes, they do now."

"I'm going to tell them. I can't lie to them, especially now we'll have a hard time avoiding each other, with you living here and all."

Tom stood from the chair and shook his head frantically, "No, no, no, Ada you can't."

"I don't want to lie to my friends, Tom. You are single, you don't have a baby. I know it won't look great, but at this stage they'll get over it," I tried to reason.

"Are you joking, Ada? You know Dena better than anyone. She will hate me, and she won't be afraid to make sure I know just how much. They've done me a great kindness, insisting I stay here. I know I've made a royal mess of things, but I'm trying to sort it all out. Please just…a few more weeks. At least wait until I move out," Tom pleaded.

I sighed, "Fine…but as soon as you move out, I'm telling her."

"Thank you, Ada," His gratitude was sincere and several seconds of silence passed whilst I sipped my coffee and I could feel his eyes still on me, "I know I shouldn't say this, but I have to. You look incredible, Ada. Pregnancy becomes you."

I scoffed, "I'm fat."

"You're radiant."

"Well, thanks…I guess."

"But I am worried about you. Especially after last night. Your wellbeing is of utmost importance to me. I know you're not going to want to hear this but…Matt was right about the caffeine," He stepped closer and gently took my mug out of my hands and set it on the counter. I opened my mouth, ready to tell him where to stick it. But he didn't let me, "I know I have no right to tell you what to do, but please listen to me and consider my advice as a healthcare professional. There have been studies into the effects of high levels of caffeine on pregnant mothers and the babies they are growing. It has been proven that it can cause low birth weight, and can increase your blood pressure, putting you at greater risk of serious pregnancy related conditions such as pre-eclampsia. As a cardiologist I also need to stress that excessive exposure to stimulants, causes an increased heart-rate in you and in the baby. I know it sounds like I'm Scaremongering, Ada, but that's not my intention, I'm saying it before I care."

"It's also been proven that going cold turkey on any addiction can do more harm than good in pregnancy."

"We aren't talking about smoking or crack cocaine, Ada," Tom's voice was suddenly very firm, "I'm asking you to cut down on the carbonated drinks and maybe switch to decaf."

I looked down at the floor and worried my bottom lip with my teeth. Suddenly I felt a bit like a child getting told off. I'd been behaving like one though. I was too stubborn for my own good, "It's really that dangerous for the baby?" I mumbled, not looking up from the floor.

"I'm not telling you all those things will happen to you, Ada. But I just want you to be aware of the dangers. I know you wouldn't want to do anything which could compromise the health of your baby. Your health is also important, as that directly affects the baby," Tom stepped a bit closer. "You aren't alone, Ada. There are lots of people who care about you."

I took a shaky breath and when I looked up, Tom was directly in front of me. So close I could smell him, a hint of sandalwood mixed with clean perspiration from his run. "Can I?" He opened his hand and let it hover over my belly.

"There's not much to feel yet."

Taking this as my permission, he stroked the tips of his fingers over my clothed stomach, "This is so precious, Ada."

I stifled a gasp as the gentle intimacy of his touch, "I…it doesn't feel real. I mean I know I'm pregnant. I've had loads of symptoms and I've seen the scan. But… it's like it's not registering. It feels like I'm watching it happen to someone else, because in my head I know it can't possibly be me. It was never me, I had so many negative tests, so many disappointments."

"It's happening, Ada," Tom reassured me, "I know there's not much I can say. But I meant what I said before. Anything you need, even if it's just someone to talk to. I'm here for you as well."

"Mmm," I nodded vaguely, because I knew that wasn't entirely true. Because he would give me everything I needed, until the day the baby arrived. Then what if what I needed was a decent night's sleep, or someone to run out in the middle of the night for nappies? He wouldn't be there then. The next nine months meant nothing, when considering all the support I'd need for the next eighteen years. But looking at Tom, he was so sincere. He looked tired, and low. No doubt stressed from everything going on in his own life. So, I decided not to say any of those thoughts out loud.

"Thank you, Tom."

CHAPTER NINE

Pink or Blue?

The email arrived in my inbox two days later. A booking for a 4D scan package in my name, at a top private clinic in London. The package consisted of three scans, a gender scan to take place after sixteen weeks, and two 4D growth scans which could be booked after twenty-four weeks. It came with printed photos and a DVD.

I'd not booked this, but I had a good idea who had.

I'd done my research in the past regarding these types of packages. They weren't cheap and I'd decided early on that there was no way I could justify spending that kind of money when there was so many more important things I'd be needing.

The email stated I'd simply have to call them to book myself in. I was already sixteen weeks, so I could find out the sex of my baby any day now. If that's what I wanted. I did want to know, but I'd accepted that I'd have to wait until my twenty-week scan. I'd only briefly considered not finding out, then decided the pregnancy its self was enough of a surprise for me.

I slipped out of the recording studio at the earliest opportunity and dialled Tom's number.

"Hello, Ada," He answered.

"Good Morning, Tom," I said, brightly, "Thank you, thank you, thank you!"

"Ah, you go the email then?"

"Yep! It's amazing, thank you! I'm going to call them in a minute."

"I'm so glad you like it, Ada. I was a bit worried you'd be cross with me for over-stepping. I just thought, after what you were saying the other day, that it might help. Seeing the baby, knowing the sex…"

"Would you like to come with me?" I anticipated him saying no. But I had to ask, because he'd paid for it. But also, otherwise I'd go alone. Dena would ask too many questions, after I'd already argued with her about nothing being able to justify the expense and my mum hated coming to London. There wasn't anyone else I considered a close enough friend to invite who would be able to keep the news to themselves.

"I'm not sure that's a good idea, Ada. Why don't you take Claudine?"

"Because she'll ask where the hell I got the money to afford it."

"Ah."

"I don't want to go alone," I knew pulling on his heart strings would work. He'd promised me he was there for me. Anything I needed. I needed him to come with me. I heard him let out a long breath as he contemplated my invite.

"I don't have patient hours on a Wednesday afternoon. If you can get an appointment after one, I'll come with you," He still sounded reluctant.

"I'm sorry, I shouldn't have asked. You don't have to, Tom. I know you're not interested –"

"No, Ada, I am interested. I'm very interested."

"Okay...so I'll text you then?"

"That'll be great."

The clinic did have an appointment available. Half past one on Wednesday.

I arranged to meet Tom outside. Fortunately, the location was central, so not far for me to travel from home, and he from work. I arrived early, the anticipation too much to bare and I hadn't been able to sit around at home a moment longer. Although I wasn't sure what I was more excited about. The scan, or the fact that Tom was coming with me.

I hadn't been disappointed when Tom first told me he couldn't be a father to my baby. I'd expected it, I'd understood, and the concept of being a single parent hadn't really hit me. But things had changed now. Tom was no longer in a relationship, he wasn't committed to fathering Grace's daughter. He obviously cared about mine and my baby's wellbeing and now he was attending the scan with me. Was is so wrong to hope? He'd made mistakes, but there was no doubt he was a good man. When it came to wanting a Daddy for my baby, I knew Tom would be a good one.

I saw him the second he turned the corner at the end of the street. He was taller than most people, so I could see his slightly unruly auburn hair over the heads of the other pedestrians on the busy London pavement. I waved as he approached.

"Hi, Ada," He stopped in front of me, taking in my appearance. We'd not seen each other since the previous Wednesday morning, when we'd had our chat in the kitchen. I'd made a conscious effort to avoid him, making plans away from the house with Dena. "I hope I didn't keep you waiting long?"

"Oh no, I was early," I told him. He was still in his work clothes, smart trousers, and this time he wore a pale pink shirt, rolled up to his elbows. He'd trimmed his beard and he looked less tired than when I last saw him. "You came straight from work?"

"Yes. My last appointment finished just before one, fortunately."

"Great, erm...shall we?" I gestured to the door, realising that things were getting a little awkward. Tom followed me silently into the entrance of the building and we approached the reception desk. It was one of those places that as soon as the door closed behind you, the noise of busy traffic was cut out, and the soft pastel paints and pleasant up-lighting turned it into the place of tranquillity.

"Good afternoon, can I help you?" The pretty blonde at the reception desk greeted us in a soft melodic tone.

"Yeah, I uh –"

"We have an appointment, for Ada Bloom, at half past one," Tom was suddenly right at my side, one hand coming to rest possessively on my lower back, whilst he put the other confidently on the top of the high oak desk.

"Thank you, just one moment," The woman tapped away on her computer. Then took a tablet from her desk drawer and prodded at the screen a couple of times, before sliding it towards us. "I can see you have an appointment booked for a gender scan. If you would both sign in here, I'll call up and let them know you've arrived."

"Thank you," Tom took the tablet and the stylus which the woman held out to him. He swiftly tapped and squiggled the screen. When he handed the tablet over to me I was surprised to see that all I had to do was put my signature in a little box. "I filled in your details," Tom said, by means of explanation. I frowned, did he not think me capable?

"That's great," the receptionist said when Tom took the tablet from me and handed it back over to her. "So, if you take to door to your left, you can take the lift or stairs to the first floor. Take a seat and you'll be called in shortly."

"Why did you do that?" I asked, as soon as we were out of earshot.

"Do what?"

"Speak for me? Fill in my details?"

In Tom's defence, he clearly didn't believe he'd done anything wrong, because he looked surprised at my annoyance, "I'm sorry, I was just... It's force of habit. I've always taken care of my girlfriends in that way. Not that you're my girlfriend...ah," realisation hit him, and I could see he was annoyed at himself.

"Oh," I pretended to ignore the girlfriend comment. We took our seats in the small, empty waiting room. After a few second of awkward silence, a funny thought hit me, and I sniggered to myself. Tom looked at me with one brow arched, so I explained. "I bet you're that guy that on dates who orders for the woman."

"Guilty," he raised one hand and let out a laugh and just like that the mood was lightened.

We didn't have to wait long, about ten minutes after we sat down the door in front of us opened and a very happy smiley couple left, followed by a tall, older woman. Her slightly grey-ing hair was tied up in a loose but tidy bun, and she had a kind smile as she addressed me. "Ada?"

"Yes," I nodded.

"Would you like to come through?" I stood up and felt Tom behind me as I greeted the woman at the doorway and she lead us into the room. It was small and like the rest of the building, painted in a pale lilac. The bed in the middle of the room was nicer than your average hospital gurney. It was a proper elec-tronic adjustable bed, with fresh white clean sheets and the lady who lead us in was just laying a fresh lilac covering over the top. "It's lovely to meet you, Ada, my name is Lilly," She turned to look at Tom, "And, are you Daddy?"

Tom and I looked at each other, clearly thinking the same thing. We'd not discussed exactly what Tom's part in this was. He was accompanying me and he was the father, but it was a compli-cated situation.

"Yes, I am," Tom eventually nodded, not taking his eyes off of mine. He smiled at me.

"Well, take a seat, Dad," She gestured to the chair next to the bed. "And Ada, if you'd like to get comfortable on the bed. Pull your top up and tuck it into your bra, and roll your leggings down below your tummy and tuck this in them, just to stop the gel going over them," She handed me a blue paper towel. I shuffled about getting comfortable and avoided looking at Tom, as I did as instructed with my clothes, and finally settled back on the bed.

"My, aren't you colourful?" Lilly grinned as she looked over my exposed flesh. "How many tattoos do you have?"

"Oh, I lost count a long time ago!" I smirked, "I doubt they'll look this good for long though, they will get all stretched and horrible soon," I ran a finger absently over the blue Peony on my right hip.

"That's a very common myth. Most abdominal tattoos return to normal after pregnancy. You're young and you have good skin," Lilly explained, and it made me smile. I'd not been worried, I always knew the risk of my body changing throughout pregnancy could change the appearance of my most favourite body art, but the news that it might not made me very happy. "So, you're Seventeen weeks and one day and you're wanting to find out the sex today is that right?"

"Yes," I nodded, and Tom remained quiet. Perhaps my earlier gripe at him speaking on my behalf causing him to watch his mouth.

"So, I've looked over your file, other than the anaemia, the pregnancy had been healthy so far. I do have to make you aware that although medically we cannot give any advice. If I do see anything of concern, I have an obligation to report it to your consultant."

"I understand," I let out a long breath, as she smiled and started setting up next to me. She set down on a little round stool with wheels and picked up the bottle of gel.

"This will feel much like your last scan. Not overly comfortable, but the image you see will be much clearer. Today we'll hopefully find out the sex, if baby is co-operating. If not, you can come back, at no additional charge. You'll get some pictures, and if I can get a good sound I'll do a recording of your baby's heartbeat on a USB stick for you to take away," Lilly explained all this, then wheeled closer, "Ready?" I grinned and nodded excitedly. I chanced a look round to Tom.

He'd been so silent that I'd almost forgotten he was sitting right next to me. He looked...nervous. He'd gone pale and he wrung his hands together. So, I did the only thing I could think of. I reached over and pried one of his clammy hands into my own.

I jumped as Lilly squeezed a blob of cold gel onto my tummy, and hissed, "Cold!" I squeaked the word.

"Sorry, I should have warned you," She apologised, as she used the wand to spread the substance around. Then the pressure increased, almost to the point of painful, as she dug the wand into my lower stomach. I was starting to wish I'd used the toilet before going in, as I very suddenly needed a wee. We couldn't see the screen yet, so I looked up at Tom again. He was staring at my stomach, almost in rapt fascination. I wasn't really showing. My hips were a bit wider, and my belly was a bit podgier.

"You're just starting to show," Lilly commented, clearly noticing Tom looking at me.

"I just feel fat at the moment," I giggled awkwardly.

"Nonsense," She shook her head. "Right, let's see," She studied the screen closer for a few moments. Her brow furrowed but not in a concerned way. "Ah here we go," She whirled the screen around to face us.

Clear as day in an odd hue of oranges was my baby. Small, and still not fully formed, but very clearly human. Little legs, with knees bent up and little arms, with tiny hands fisted up and resting either side of it's head.

"Oh..." I breathed out the word, as the tiny human of the screen kicked its legs and moved a hand to its mouth, in what looked like a thumb sucking motion. It was then I felt Tom's hand tighten on mine. I peered round to see him staring intently at the screen, a new look I hadn't seen on him before adorned his features. Adoration?

"So, the moment of truth. Let's have a look and find out if this little one is pink or blue," Lilly grinned at us and moved the wand a little more, whilst she tapped on the computer, until the image zoomed in. "There we are. I can tell you, without a doubt you are most definitely having a little boy. Congratulations Mummy and Daddy!"

A boy. *I'm having a baby boy.*

"Are...are you certain?" Tom's voice was croaky, and unsure. When I turned to look at him, I was surprised to see tears brimming in his eyes.

"Normally we say we can never be one hundred percent, but here I'll show you. Right here, you can see his formed testis. It's an unobstructed picture, because he's dancing his little legs up right now. He's a very active little fella, have you felt any movement yet?" Lilly directed her question at me.

"No...well...I've thought I've felt flutters, I'm not sure."

"Well it won't be long. He's big too, long legs, like his daddy," She grinned at Tom, "From his measurements he's already weighing around eleven ounces. To give you a rough idea, ten ounces is average at twenty weeks."

I felt Tom pull my hand up and I looked at him again when his lips grazed my knuckles. I couldn't help but beam at him.

"I'm going to see if we can get some good sound and listen to his heart, then I can do the recording for you," a few more taps at the keyboard and a familiar whooshing that I'd heard at the midwife appointment a week prior filled the air. Then a beating, "That's you," She explained, and Tom nodded, knowingly. Then a second beat could be heard, a faster one, thundering along like a little train, "That's it, your little mans heartbeat, I'll leave that on for a minute for you both to listen to, whilst I go and sort your pictures and recording out."

I watched the screen for a moment longer, mesmerised by my baby wriggling about, whilst I could hear his rapid little heart beating away. Tom was now holding my hand with both of his, still pressing it to his mouth, placing a little kiss on it every now and again.

"Are you alright?" I asked. He didn't answer me for a moment, just stared past me at the screen. His eyes were red and I could hear that his breathing was shaky. "Do you need to go outside?"

"No," He answered, turning his attention to me. "I just didn't expect... I can't believe how incredible this is. A boy..."

"It's odd, I feel ridiculously happy about the fact that I'm having a boy, but I know I'd have felt the same, had she said girl. It just... it feels... I dunno?"

"Real?"

"Yes...it feels so real."

*

We left the clinic together and when we stepped onto the pavement, Tom turned to me. "Do you have to be anywhere?"

"Erm, no?"

"Have you eaten?" I shook my head, "Did you want to get some late lunch?"

"What do you have in mind?" I asked, expecting him to suggest sandwich and a drink in Starbucks.

"Do you like burgers?" He shot an arm out and wrapped it round my waist, pulling me out of the way when a crowd of pedestrians passed us.

"Are you taking me to McDonalds?" I arched an eyebrow.

"Well if you like...but I was thinking of this great American style diner not too far from here. I could kill for a massive bacon and cheese burger, with chips and onion rings," That did sound good, although I wasn't sure sharing lunch was the best idea. But my suddenly grumbling stomach got the better of me.

"That sounds amazing. I'm in!"

A short walk later we were seated in the window of, as Tom had described, an American Diner in the middle of London. Complete with US sports memorabilia adorning the walls, straw dispensers and fake mini Juke Boxes on each table. The waiting staff wore short little skirts with tucked in shirts and neck scarfs – all they were missing were roller skates.

"What are you drinking?" Tom asked, looking over his menu at me.

"Mmm Pepsi, Pepsi, Pepsi... I'll have a mineral water...and a banana milkshake."

"Good girl," Tom laughed, "I think I'll have the same, but chocolate."

"Think I'm going to have the buttermilk chicken burger, with bacon and cheese fries," I pondered my own menu, turning it in my hands.

"Sound good, I'm still going for the bacon and cheese burger, regular fries, and onion rings, do you want onion rings?" Tom set his menu down on the table.

"I do...but I'll probably regret it, maybe get a large portion to share?" He nodded in agreement. Just then a waitress came over and we gave our orders, and I couple help but giggle as Tom consciously made sure not to order for me, when he gestured to me, so I could speak first.

"So...a boy," Tom smiled across the table at me, "Were you expecting it, did you have a gut feeling?"

"Not at all, people kept asking me. But no, no gut feeling. My mum will be gutted, I think she was hoping for a granddaughter. My brother has a boy," I explained. The waiter returned and put our drinks in front of us. I took a long drag of my milkshake through the draw. "I love these kinds of places."

"You can't beat a big greasy burger."

"Says the heart doctor, aren't you worried about clogging your arteries with all that saturated fat?" I teased.

"Hilarious, Ada. I'll have you know that I run five miles a day, so I can allow myself to eat whatever the hell I want."

"You're crazy!"

"I enjoy running."

"Like I just said. You're crazy," I laughed, before gazing around the little diner thoughtfully, "Better in America though. I mean these places are quite novel, but nothing beats the real thing. I expect you've spent a fair bit of time over there, what with Grace being American and all…"

"Less time than you'd think. I work a lot, but we spent three weeks over there last summer, but that was actually a family holiday in Florida with my Mum, Sisters and Nieces. It was really good fun…and yes we ate a lot of burgers." He chuckled, "Have you spent much time over there?"

"Only half of my life. My brother lives in California with his wife and my nephew. My Dad, well he's retired now, but he still owns two recording studios over there. So, I spent a lot of my school summer holidays at work with my Dad. I loved it." I beamed at the memory.

"That's how you got into music?" I nodded. "So where are you actually from? Not London?"

"Brighton, my parents still live there. You?"

"Originally Wimbledon, then Oxfordshire."

"Posh boy."

"Yep," Tom laughed.

"I bet you went to boarding school," It was a joke, one I knew I could make.

"I did," He was laughing now, and I could see his cheeks turning slightly pink, he covered his face with his hands, feigning embarrassment.

"Me too," Tom dropped his hands, and stared at me. He looked like he'd just swallowed his tongue.

"You went to boarding school?"

"Don't sound so surprised. I just told you my Dad owned two recording studios in the states. My parents travelled a lot, they didn't want mine and my brother's educations to suffer," I explained. Then I laughed, "Believe it or not, I was a star student, head girl, captain of the netball team, I was a goody two-shoes."

"No that makes complete sense, I just wasn't expecting it," Tom stopped as our food arrived. "So, your Mum and Dad are still together?"

"I know, a rarity these days isn't it? But yeah, they have quite a weird relationship. When I was younger Dad was away a lot and I think it kind of kept their relationship exciting, always missing each other. Now Dad's at home all the time, but they live separate lives. They love each other to bits, but Dad has his things, Mum has hers."

"Whatever works for them I guess," Tom smiled at me, "You must miss your brother. One of my sisters lives in New Zealand, we talk all the time, but I miss her like crazy."

"I do. I miss my nephew. Seeing him grow up. My brother wants to get home for when this one comes along," I gestured to my belly, "He texts me nearly every day for updates. He's really excited."

"I'm sure."

I realised I may have hit a sore point. My family's excitement over the baby. Tom had told no one, for obvious reasons. But I knew after his reaction today that when he said he cared he really meant it. He wasn't supporting me financially out of a sense of obligation. He didn't feel able to commit to parenthood, and as much as part of me hoped he might change his mind, I wasn't about to force him. But he was doing the best he could the only way he knew how.

"How is your burger?" I decided to divert the topic.

"Too good."

"So where are you moving to? Dena said your new place wasn't ready?"

"Not too far from them actually. A little two bed ground floor flat in a converted townhouse. It needed a little bit of work. There's no water...or electric. Or a functioning kitchen. But it will all be sorted by the end of next week I hope, well enough for me to start moving my things in and getting settled."

"Are you excited?"

"It's bitter sweet. I really liked my old house. I'd have stayed there if I could have."

"I know what you mean."

"But it will be nice to have my own space again. I appreciate Matt and Claudine's hospitality, but feel like I'm getting under their feet."

"Don't be ridiculous."

"Alright, I miss the peace and quiet of my own company, is that any better?" I laughed at his admission.

"Dena can be a bit full on."

"She's wonderful. Just… yeah alright, really full on."

I laughed, "Don't worry, I won't tell her that you hate her."

"I never said that!"

"Yeah, alright," I was quickly learning that Tom was fun to wind up. He was sensitive in his own way, and he cared what people thought of him.

Thoroughly stuffed with burgers and milkshake Tom got the bill, and we left together. Without discussion we both headed for the closest tube station and caught the Northern Line together. Our light-hearted conversation continued until the onboard tannoy announced the train was approaching Chalk Farm and Tom stood up.

"You'll be okay the rest of the way?" Tom asked, reaching to touch the top of my arm.

"Of course."

"Well…this is me."

"Okay…well, erm…thanks. For today, for lunch. I had a really nice time, Tom," I sat in my seat a little awkwardly. We had, had a really nice time, but now I wasn't sure how we were ending things. To my surprise Tom leant back down, resting one knee on the empty seat next to me and wrapped his arms around me. It took me a second to react, but I returned his embrace.

"I had a great time too, Ada. Take care of yourself for me."

He let go of me as the train came to a complete stop and he

gripped onto the overhead bar to steady himself. With one last smile, he jumped off the train and left me to complete my journey alone.

CHAPTER TEN

Hopes diminished

Twenty Weeks

I should have known better than to get my hopes up. I tried not to be too affected by the fact that I'd not heard a word from Tom since our lovely afternoon together following the scan. I'd seen him once at Dena's, he'd passed the sitting room, to the kitchen to make himself a drink before disappearing back to his room. Dena said he was working, but I didn't buy it. There had been another lump of money deposited into my bank account, but I was so cross by the fact that he'd not so much as text me to see how I was, that I didn't bother to thank him.

I knew why. I'd put too much pressure on him. I should never have asked him to accompany me. We got too familiar, and it had always been a silent agreement that we shouldn't. He'd made his stance very clear and despite taking no parental responsibility, he'd been honest and fair. He'd not messed me around. I'd known where I stood. Now I didn't. That was my fault, not his. Because I'd allowed myself to get carried away.

Was it so wrong to like the father of my child? To enjoy his company, to still find him attractive? Because that was the truth. I didn't just want him to father my child, I wanted him to like me. To want me. But that could just be the hormones talking. I'd been horny as hell for weeks and my mind spent a lot of time fixating on my last sexual encounter.

I felt like a school girl with a crush. I wanted Tom to speak to me. I wanted to have lunch again and be in his company. I'd pulled him up on his controlling behaviour at the scan, but part of me wanted that. Yearned to have a man who would just take care of everything. It was old fashioned and although Magnus had made me feel safe and protected, it was in a totally different way.

Magnus was a brute of a man. His Scandinavian roots obvious in his Viking like stature. He stood at six foot five, fair hair, blue eyes and built like a brick shit house. His presence in a room was over-bearing and no one in their right minds would mess with him. I used to find that exciting.

Now I'd been shown a different sort of protection. A careful consideration of my feelings and my needs. Tom's approach was gentler and he was fully in control of all situations.

I wanted him to look after me.

"Are you alright?" I jumped at Dena's voice. We were curled up in the booth of a little pub not far from the hospital. I'd had my twenty-week scan and she'd accompanied me. I'd been told once again, that I was having a boy. Dena still had no idea about the earlier sexing scan I'd attended with Tom, and the lies were getting deeper. I had feigned excitement and surprise in front of her when the sonographer at the hospital revealed what I was having.

The woman had backed up Lilly's words. The baby was big, larger than average but it was all in the legs. I should expect to have a very long baby. Everything still looked healthy and as it should.

I'd hoped all week that Tom might message me to wish me luck or to make sure I let him know how things were. He knew the scan was due. But I'd not heard a peep.

"Yeah, I'm alright. Just tired."

"We can go home. We don't have to stay out," Dena looked sympathetic. I did get tired very quickly these days and she'd come to accept that I needed more rest. My body was working hard.

"It's fine."

"Tom moved out, you'll be relieved to know. So, you don't have to make excuses not to hang out at ours anymore," I nearly choked at her words.

"I have no idea what you mean!"

"I'm not stupid, Ada. You clearly don't like the guy. The only time you ever avoid people is when you can't stand them."

"I don't have a problem with Tom."

"You do. The last few weeks you've been acting really weird. Whenever you're at ours you're on tender hooks. Whenever his name comes up, you go all tense…just like you are now!"

"Honestly. I just feel your place is a bit crowded right now. Also, I'm making the most of going out whilst I still can. In a couple of month's I won't be able to just go for dinner, or the cinema."

"That's all well and good, but it doesn't explain how awkward you are around him."

"He's fine. I hardly know him."

Dena quieted down but didn't stop looking at me as a sipped my Cranberry juice. Her eyes narrowed, and she made a 'Hmm' noise. "What?" I shot at her, a little exasperated by the topic of conversation. I didn't want to talk about Tom. I didn't want to keep lying to her.

"Oh...my...god..."

"What?" I practically shouted, before lowering my voice, and speaking again, "What's wrong with you?"

"You fancy him!" She pointed an accusatory finger at me and let out a giggle. "You fancy Tom!"

"I do not!" my response was a little overly indignant.

"You so do, you're going red!" My hands flew to my cheeks and sure enough they were warm.

"I don't fancy Tom, Dena. Don't be ridiculous. Like I said I don't even know the bloke."

"You don't have to know him to want to get in his pants!"

"That's disgusting!" I wasn't sure why that thought offended me so much. Because that's exactly what I had done. Slept with him, without knowing anything about him. Other than the fact that he was a doctor and he had been in a relationship at the time.

"I can have a chat with Matt if you like, see if he'll put a good word in. I'm not sure if he'll go for it though. You know what with you being up the duff and all. Not to mention the mess with Grace. Don't think he'd make that mistake ag..." Dena trailed off, realising she'd shared something she shouldn't have. Not that I didn't already know, but she didn't know that. She shrugged, "He's probably pretty horny though, he might be up for a shag."

"You will not speak to Matt. You won't repeat a word of this conversation to anyone! I don't fancy, Tom. I don't have a problem with him. Drop it!"

"Jesus! Pregnancy has killed your sense of humour."

"There is nothing wrong with my sense of humour. You weren't joking, so there's nothing to laugh at."

"Alright, alright, I get your point. I'm sorry," Dena relented and offered and small smile, then she grinned, "There's worse people you could crush on though, Tom is *hung*!"

I almost sprayed my mouthful of juice across the table and ended up coughing as I forced myself to swallow it a bit too quickly. I gasped to get my breath back, "How the fuck would you know?"

I might not have been so shocked at her statement, if I hadn't known she was right. Tom was *hung*. Well, certainly larger than average. I may have been drunk, but I clearly remembered my surprise at Tom's body beneath his clothes. I knew his cock was just as lovely as the rest of him.

"Well...you can just tell. He wears those sport shorts when he goes running, they leave nothing to the imagination. Plus, the other day I may have accidently seen him getting undressed..." She trailed off, and I raised an eyebrow.

"Accidently?"

"He left the bedroom door open!" Dena defended herself, "I'm a woman, I don't care if I'm married, I see an attractive, naked man, in *my* house no less…I'm going to look."

"You're wrong on so many levels, Dena."

"You still love me."

"Always…pervert."

*

I perched on the edge of my bed, mobile phone in hand, and my thumb hovered over the send button.

The afternoon with Dena had given me a lot to think about. I needed her. I couldn't lose her. More now than ever. I had to think what was more important to me. Right now, it was making sure I didn't risk my friendship with her. The lie was too deep and I knew if I told her now, she'd hate me.

It wasn't just a lie about the paternity of my unborn child anymore. I'd omitted to tell her about the gender scan. I'd also outrightly lied when she asked if I had a problem with Tom. And then strongly denied the accusation that I fancied him.

None of that was part of the agreement when I told Tom I wouldn't tell her he was the father straight away. It's a well-known fact that lies easily get out of hand and this one had spiralled right out of control. There was no way out of it without completely breaking my best friends heart.

I'm not telling Dena.

I hit send.

No hello, no kisses, no explanation.

It didn't take long for my phone to start ringing. It was Tom. I answered the call.

"Hi, Tom."

"Ada, what's happened?"

"Nothings happened. Dena's just... it's gone on too long. I'm in too deep. I think it's for the best that she and Matt don't find out."

"Right..."

"I mean, it's not going to make any difference is it? You aren't going to be around."

"Ada –"

"So, why upset everyone by telling them something which is doesn't really matter. What they don't know can't hurt them. It will be better for the baby too. In the long run...no one knowing," I finished, and Tom was quiet on the other end of the line for a few seconds.

"I'm so sorry, Ada. I didn't mean for it to turn out like this."

"I'm not sure how you did expect it to turn out?"

"I needed to back off, I can't... I've fucked up so bad, Ada. I'm scared of fucking up even more, I don't want to put that on you, or on him, he doesn't deserve it," *Him.* He was talking about the baby.

"I'd would never stop you being part of his life, Tom."

"I know you wouldn't. That's the problem. I'm not good enough for him, or for you. You both deserve better."

That was when I realised. Tom's decision not to have an active role in his son's life had nothing to do with not wanting to. His issues were much deeper. What had happened with Grace had severely affected him, he'd lost his sense of self-worth. In his mind, Grace had not deemed him good enough to be a father to her child.

He believed this to be the result of his infidelity. In part, perhaps it was. Grace was likely scared he wouldn't stay around, he would abandon her eventually, and she'd be left alone. So, she pushed him away for self-preservation.

But in truth. Their relationship had been over the moment she discovered she was pregnant with another mans child. Tom may be the most kind-hearted man in the world, but that child would never have been his and he would never have been able to truly love it as his own. Grace wouldn't have allowed him, she wasn't able to allow him to love her.

I also knew that me trying to tell him otherwise would be futile.

"I'm sorry I pushed you, by asking you to come to the scan with me. I know you've made your decision. I don't hate you for it. If we see each other, I don't want things to be awkward."

"Me neither."

"It's better this way."

"I know you're right."

We both fell silent. I felt sad for Tom, and for my baby boy. But also, for myself, because I knew any hopes that I had that Tom might change his mind, were over. I was on my own.

"For what it's worth, I know you're a good man. I think we'd both be very lucky to have you."

"You'll keep me informed, won't you? I want to know that you are well. I would like to know when he arrives."

"If that's what you want, of course I will."

"Thank you. You're a good girl, Ada."

"Bye, Tom."

"Bye, Ada."

CHAPTER ELEVEN

A recipe for disaster

24 weeks

I suppose you could say my life had returned to some kind of normalcy. Well as normal as it could get, whilst being pregnant and knowing in just sixteen weeks, give or take a few days, my whole world would be turned on its head.

But I'd found a routine. I'd settled down. I'd accepted what was happening and that I'd be doing it alone. Of course, I'd have the support of my family, and Dena and Matt. But I'd still be a single mother. I was alright with that. I didn't really have a choice but to be okay with it.

My little flat was slowly filling with baby related stuff. Matt had come over and helped me rearrange my bedroom to create room for a changing table and Moses basket. The table was set up, but the basket was still wrapped in its cellophane, balanced upon its stand. My Dad had driven up one weekend and taken me shopping for some space saving furniture. So now my clothes had been transferred into a more compact wardrobe, and a second set of drawers was now starting to fill up with little vests and baby grows.

I'd even brought a pram. It was horrifically expensive, and I'd been shocked to discover a) the complexity of selecting the right mode of transport for my child, and b) how much these shops knew people would pay. It was all getting very expensive and I was suddenly pleased for the money Tom was giving me. I'd have managed without it, it would have been tight, and if I'd been desperate I know my parents would help me out, they certainly weren't hurting for money, but I hated to ask. I'd always been self-sufficient, I'd never asked my family for a penny. But I didn't feel bad using Tom's money, he was the baby's father after all.

Tom had kept in touch with me, since we had our little heart to heart those weeks ago. He was regularly texting me to see how I was. I'd just been for my first 4D growth scan at the clinic alone, and he text me on the day to ask me to let him know how it went. Which I did. The texts had become easier, now I knew exactly where we stood again, it was easier to push my feelings aside. I knew right now the only important thing was my baby. That's where I was focusing all my attention.

The only thing I was yet to do, was tell Magnus that I was pregnant.

I'd been avoiding it. I'd even contacted the bands manager and pulled out of working on their next album. I told him it was because I'd find it too difficult working that closely with Mag's. No one argued it. I'd known the band a long time and it had been weird for everyone when our relationship had ended. I don't think they would have been surprised at my pulling out of the album.

My work was slowing down anyway and that was a purposeful effort. Contracts were coming to an end and I was not taking on new work. All I had was one twelve-month deal with a studio who were now fully aware of my pregnancy and they'd kindly agreed to push my start date back to six months after the baby was born. Giving me time to adapt to parenthood and be fully on board with them. Fortunately, I had a strong resume and was known in the industry, so I was lucky enough that most employers would adapt to my requirements.

For the first time in ages, Dena and Matt had suggested a night at one of our old haunts. A pub not far from Canary Wharf called 'The Flying Dutchman' it did Karaoke on the first Friday of every month and we used to be regulars. We hadn't been for a long time, not since before Mags and I broke up. But I was keen to enjoy my last weeks of freedom, and I'd not sung for a long time. I also wanted an excuse to buy a new dress. My clothes were becoming increasingly tight, and I was fed up with making do.

I was waiting at the bus stop to go straight from the city to Dena's to get ready when my phone rang. Her smiley display picture filled the screen, and I answered the call.

"I'm at the bus stop, I'll be like half an hour."

"That's fine."

"Okay," I frowned, wondering why the hell she was calling. Then my bus appeared at the end of the road, "Hang on, I'm just going to get on the bus I'll call you back."

The bus stopped, and I got on, swiping my Oyster Card and taking advantage of one of the seat at the front with a sign stating they were reserved for the Elderly and Pregnant woman. I shoved my shopping bags at my feet and called her back.

"That was quick."

"I get priority seating these days," She laughed.

"So… you know how a few weeks ago you said you didn't have a problem with Tom, and you definitely didn't fancy him?"

"I recall the conversation," I feigned disinterest, but I had a horrible feeling as to where this was going.

"I thought that you wouldn't mind if he tagged along with us tonight."

I tried not to hesitate too much, "No, I'm not bothered."

"Thank god. Matt invited him without telling me, and he's on his way over. I think Matt didn't fancy being the third wheel tonight."

"Matt the third wheel?" I giggled at the thought, "Does Tom know I'm coming?"

"I don't think so, Matt didn't tell him it was Karaoke, he just asked him to come out for drinks. I think he got used to the male company and misses having him around."

"Bless."

"Oh, and I've ordered Pizza."

"Amazing, I'm famished."

"See you in a bit."

"Bye babes." I hung up. Then immediately tapped out a text to Tom.

I take it Matt omitted to tell you that I'm coming tonight? x

It didn't take long to get a reply.

First I've heard. Are we alright? x

I'm alright if you are? X

It will be good to see you Ada. x

I shoved my phone back into my bag. At least giving him fore-warning would stem any initial awkwardness. But part of me was excited. He said it would be 'good to see me' and that dimin-ished hope found another little spark deep in my belly. I wanted to see him, and I wanted him to see me. There was a tiny part of me that considered it was probably a terrible idea and that I should have told him to make an excuse and pull out of tonight. It would look less suspect him changing his mind, than me. But then there was the part of me that remembered his handsome face and how very sweet he was, and how utterly besotted I really was with him.

It suddenly seemed like four weeks of me carrying on as if everything was fine was for naught. I was right back to where I started.

*

"Look at you, I think I married the wrong woman," Matt jested when I entered the kitchen. We'd eaten, then Dena and I had dis-appeared upstairs to get ready to go out. Dena was still faffing around with her curling Iron.

"Don't let her hear you say that, Matthew…Hi, Tom."

"Ada," Tom tilted his bottle of beer towards me in greeting, from his seat at the breakfast bar. He'd not been there when I'd arrived a little bit earlier on in the evening. Dena had said he was getting ready at home before coming over as he only lived around the corner.

He looked good, in black slim fit jeans and a grey tee shirt. It was basically a newer, less battered version of what I'd seen him in before, on his non-working and not attending a wedding days. But overall he looked great, less tired, happier and heathier than the last time I'd actually seen him, almost seven weeks ago.

"Excuse me a minute, I'm going to get changed now you're down here to entertain Tom," Matt slipped from his stool and brushed by me, grinning as he did. Dena had definitely told him about our conversation. I could tell by his teasing expression as he left the room.

Tom and I remained silent until we heard Matt reach the top of the stairs, and then we both fought for the first word.

"I'm sorry, if I'd known –"

"I'm really glad that –"

"It's so good to see –"

We both stopped and then I couldn't stifle the giggle that escaped my lips. Tom smiled and we both laughed.

"You look great, Ada."

"You look good too, you don't look quite so tired."

"I'm not sure how I should take that?"

"Oh, definitely as a compliment," I smirked, and felt my cheeks warm up under his gaze. His gaze which travelled from my face to my stomach and lingered there. There was no mistaking that

I was pregnant now. I wasn't wearing a maternity dress, but the design gathered at the empire line and the excess material flowed down to just above the knee, and skimmed gently over my swollen belly, making my bump more obvious than normal. I stroked my hand over my belly. "No hiding it now."

"No," Tom shook his head, "Does he...have you felt him move yet?"

"Oh yeah, loads!" I nodded eagerly, "He's not strong enough to feel on the outside yet, but most of the time it feels like he's doing somersaults. He goes a bit mad if I drink anything too cold, or eat something sweet,"

"And you're feeling well?"

"Yep, they've taken me off the iron tablets at last, I thought I might have to stay on them the whole way through. The midwife said I'm a picture of health," I grinned proudly.

"That's really, really good news... you know I thought this might be awkward."

"Me too."

"I really want to... would it be okay if I gave you a hug? I just feel so horrible for how I've behaved and I've thought about you so much," Tom slipped from his stool and took a hesitant step towards me.

"I think that would be okay? I mean...what's the worse that could happen? I'm already pregnant," I snorted and Tom shook his head, his shoulders shaking with laughter as he enveloped me in his arms and pulled me close.

It felt nice. I realised we'd never actually had a proper cuddle.

Not the night we slept together, not since then. Unless you counted the night he had held me, when I first found out I was pregnant, or our brief embrace on the train after my scan. Tom's long arms wrapped all the way around my shoulders and he held me securely against his solid body. He was warm and he smelt incredible. A natural masculine musk, with a hint of sandal-wood.

But it ended all too soon when we heard Dena's heels clicking across the hardwood floor and we reluctantly pulled away from each other.

"Right, Taxi's on the way!" Dena announced loudly, before turn-ing around in the doorway of the kitchen and screaming back up the stairs. "Matt, hurry the fuck up!"

*

"So, let me get this straight...." The four of us were squeezed into a tiny booth at the back of the busy pub and Tom currently had the karaoke folder open in front of him. "It shouldn't be a ser-ious choice, I'm not expected to get up there and belt out Bohe-mian Rhapsody like Freddy Mercury, but I do have to sing."

"You have to," Dena nodded, "It's the rules, VIRGIN!"

I rolled my eyes, she was only on her second drink, but ever the lightweight, Dena was already well on her way.

"I can't believe you've never done Karaoke before," I was still shocked that someone could reach the ripe old age of thirty-seven and not have even seen someone else do Karaoke, let alone take part.

"Apparently, I haven't lived," Tom grinned at me and turned back to the book, flipping a few more pages, then he looked at

Dena, "What are you singing?"

"She's not allowed to sing," Matt started, "She's tone deaf."

"How do you know I'm not?" Tom looked hopeful. There might be a chance he would not have to embarrass himself.

"I've heard you sing, Tom. In the car, in the shower, at the Rugby, now choose a fucking song already, before I choose one for you," Matt grabbed at the folder playfully, and Tom held onto it, the pair of them scrabbled over it for a moment, before Tom won out, and got it back.

"Ada will sing Total Eclipse of the Heart, she always does," Dena told Tom, very matter of factly.

"Or Cabaret, I do a great Sally Bowls," I reminded her, "And Matt and I always do a duet…what are you thinking, stud?"

Matt smirked at my little nickname for him, remembering our hilarious rendition of 'You're the One that I want' that we'd sang whilst on holiday a couple of years back. "I've got a few thoughts, but your ideas are normally better than mine."

"Well, I know we've done it loads, but I always enjoy 'Don't you want me?' so that's my vote," I offered up my choice for the obligatory duet.

"Okay, well I'm going to throw in a curve ball, we've not done this one before…'Don't go breaking my heart'," Matt looked around the table expectantly.

Dena grinned and clapped her hands, and Tom was smirking. I could feel my head moving in a nodding motion, "Matt you utter genius, go put our names down now…and put me down for Total Eclipse,"

"And me...for... ugh, if I'm going to make a tit of myself I might as well push the boat out, put me down for 'Don't Stop Believing'," Tom shook his head, as if he didn't quite believe he had just made that choice.

"Good lad!" Matt jeered, and he headed off to put our names down.

*

Tom collapsed back into the booth, the cheers and whooping that followed him off stage in the immediate aftermath of his performance slowly dying down. He slid along the padded leather seat next to me and squeezed up closer than I was expecting. The feeling of his long lean thigh pressed up against my softer one took me quite by surprise, but I tried to ignore it. Instead opting to praise his efforts.

"Tom! You were fantastic!" I beamed at him.

"Man, you're wasting your talents in that hospital," Matt stood from the opposite side of the booth, giving Tom a firm pat on the shoulder.

"I need another drink," Tom momentarily covered his face with both his hands and dragged his palms down as he exhaled. "I can't believe I just fucking did that!"

"Did you see everyone? Everyone was singing along. They loved you!" Dena bounced in her seat. "You have to do another song."

"No way," Tom shook his head, and wrapped a hand around his empty glass and I jumped in my seat as I felt his other hand, the one closest to me, slip over my knee and up to my thigh, giving it a gentle squeeze. But he didn't look at me, instead he tilted the glass towards Matt. "You going to the bar then?"

"I am, same again?" Matt asked Tom first, then he looked at me and Dena. Dena just nodded and sipped at what was left in her own glass.

"I'll just have water...oh, but could you see if they have any Mini Cheddars behind the bar?" I asked, my stomach suddenly hinting at me that it needed sustenance immediately.

"Mini cheddars?" Matt arched his brow.

"Yes, or better yet see if they are still serving food? Maybe they do a cheese board or something?" That thought suddenly seemed incredibly appealing. Yes, a cheese board was exactly what I needed right now.

"Erm... Ada? Seriously? I'm not asking if they can make you a cheese board at..." Matt looked at his watch, "Ten past ten at night!"

"Matt, the girl wants a cheeseboard, you'll fucking well ask for one," Dena's voice was slurring a little.

"No...no it's fine, you're right..." I hesitated, "Just Mini Cheddars, or cheese and onion crisps," I felt my shoulders drop.

Matt chuckled and shook his head, before turning to the bar and I watched him stumble a little, the effects the alcohol seeping through slowly. He'd always been able to hold it the best out of all of us.

"Cheese?"

"Hmm?" I turned to look at Tom.

"Why do you want cheese?" He asked, his fingers still wrapped over my thigh and pressed in gently as he asked his question. I wondered if I should move his hand. But he wasn't really doing any harm.

"She started getting this craving about a week ago," Dena started to explain, before I could, "Cheese this, cheese that. I phoned her the other night and she was eating a plate of cheese for dinner."

"It wasn't just cheese!" I defended myself, "I had some grapes with it."

Dena almost snorted before slipping out of the booth, "I'm going to the loo," She announced louder than necessary, before disappearing through the crowd.

This was my chance to slide along a bit and put some space between me and Tom. But instead I just stayed where I was. Letting him continue to…basically grope my leg. When I looked at Tom he was staring at me with fond eyes and a tiny smile gracing his lips.

"How drunk are you?" I found myself asking.

"Am I embarrassing myself that much that you need to ask?" Tom laughed. He didn't actually seem too drunk. He wasn't slurring and he seemed aware of himself, especially his hand which had crept a little higher up my leg. But his dilated pupils and flushed cheeks gave him away.

"No," I shook my head, chuckling. "But I don't think completely sober you would be feeling me up under the table quite so keenly."

"I'm sorry," the words left his mouth, but he didn't move his hand. Instead he leant over and his other hand landed softly on my belly and stroked over it. I wasn't sure what to do. I knew really, I should push his hands away. This was bound to end badly. Especially if Dena and Matt were to see what was going on. But then part of me was enjoying it. Not just his attentions to my bump and the baby, but the warmth of his hand on my thigh, even through the fabric of my dress. If I wasn't pregnant, if I was a bit drunk and if this was any other situation, which involved me and Tom, I knew I'd be spreading my legs wider and just begging him to touch me.

That thought snapped me out of it. Despite the burning heat in the pit of my stomach, brought on by his attentions, I gently pushed both his hands from me. "Please stop," I asked him softly and he nodded, pouting a little, but he did stop, nonetheless.

Just seconds before Matt placed a tray of drinks down on the table, accompanied by two packets of Mini Cheddars.

*

I was just on the last big chorus of my chosen song when I knew, what had surprisingly turned out to be a very enjoyable night so far, was about to go completely down the pan.

I was thankful I'd got through my big note. As per usual I had most of the patrons on their feet, waving their arms above their heads, singing along to the Bonnie Tyler classic. But I almost stumbled over the closing bars when I saw a very familiar head towering above most others and making its way through the crowd, heading in the direction of my little group of friends.

I tried not to watch as Magnus got Matt's attention with the firm pat to the shoulder. But I couldn't help it. Matt turned and

I could see the surprise on his face, as they joined hands and pulled together for a manly hug and slap on the back. Then Dena's distaste at seeing him, as she reluctantly let him kiss her on the cheek. Then he looked at the stage, directly at me and I was pleased my song was over, because my mouth had dried up so much, I wasn't sure I'd be able to get another note out.

I quickly thanked the applauding crowd and hopped down from the stage. I tried to escape to the loos, but Dena's grip on my wrist slowed me down, "Mags is here."

"I know, I saw," I told her, and bit my lip.

"Shitting hell, Ada. You haven't told him, have you?"

"Not yet."

"You said you were going to tell him, you hadn't mentioned it since, I just thought you'd done it and didn't want to talk about it."

"I tried..."

"Not very hard apparently."

"I did, I picked up the phone so many times. But I just...couldn't. I...I pulled out of the album. So, I don't have to work with him," My shoulders dropped, realising I'd made everything so much worse, than it would have been, had I just called Magnus and told him weeks ago.

"For fucks sake, Ada," Dena shook her head and stepped closer to me, wrapping her arms around my shoulders. She gave me a tight squeeze. "You should have told me. Come on, let's go and face the music."

I nodded and reluctantly followed my friend back through the busy bar room to our table. Mags and Matt were chatting away, Tom was nowhere in sight, I assumed he'd gone to the toilet. Or maybe gone home. Whatever, I was pleased he wasn't here for this.

"Ada!" Magnus saw me and immediately broke his attention away from Matt to approach me.

"Hi."

"Fancy seeing you here."

"Well, it's been a while you know."

"I do," It had been so long since I'd seen him in person, even longer since I'd really spoken to him. He was so…gorgeous. He really was, just so big and tall. And his voice, his accented words had always driven me mad.

We were both quiet for a moment and I watched him eye me up and down, drinking me in. I knew I looked different. I was waiting for him to realise.

"You look well, Ada."

"Erm…thanks. So, do you."

"Yeah well, I don't feel it, I had to fly back from Germany early and cut the tour short so I could meet with a new producer, because ours let us down…"

"I'm sorry, Mags…"

"It's fine, Ada. I get it. It's a pain the backside, but I do understand." Magnus reached out, opening his arms. It was a move I knew well and I shirked away, a little too quickly. I could not have his hands on me, I could not let him hug me.

"It's just been really hard, you know. I should have given you more notice, but I put it off to be honest and I just didn't think I could face working with you every day. I've got so much going on at the moment and it took me a really long time to stop hurting..."

"Yeah well, the heartbreak doesn't seem to have affected your appetite too much," It was a biting comment and it didn't surprise me. Magnus could be spiteful when he was pissed off, and clearly my refusal to work with the band had affected him. But his comment regarding my size shook me. I stood in stunned silence and my mouth fell open. I was so shocked, that I didn't flinch when I felt a warm hand rest on my lower back.

"Is this man bothering you?" Oh, fucking, shit. Tom stood close to me now and he was shooting daggers at Magnus.

"Who the fuck do you think you are?" Magnus looked livid at being reduced to 'this man' and the insinuation that he might be 'bothering me'.

"I'd like to ask the same question to the man who has just had the cheek to call my friend fat...she's pregnant mate and you are clearly upsetting her, so if you don't mind, I think it's about time you fucked the hell off and left her alone," Tom attempted to steer me away and I foolishly hoped for a split second, that Magnus might just let it go and leave.

But his big hand around my wrist, pulling me out of Tom's hold and back to face him, put that idea to rest very quickly. Magnus looked like he was stuck between wanting to vomit and wanting to smash something up.

"Who the fuck is this guy, Ada? He's fucking delusional, because I know he's lying," Magnus' angry blue eyes were storming, as he searched my face for an explanation. Tom was on my heels. Magnus shot him a look over my shoulder, "You can stay right there and let her answer me."

"He's not lying, Mags," I said the words quietly and could see Dena, edging closer, eyes filled with concern and Matt coming up to Tom, trying to pull him away.

"I think you should let go of her, Magnus, mate," Matt stepped a bit closer and gestured to where his hand was still fastened tightly around my wrist and he let go quickly. I immediately put my hand over my stomach in a protective gesture and stroked over my bump. The action made the fabric of my dress stretch over my swollen belly and suddenly my pregnancy was very obvious to him.

"I don't... how fucking could you?" the words that left Magnus' mouth were tinged with pain and his eyes suddenly filled with hate, "Is this him?" he threw an accusatory finger over in Tom's direction. I couldn't see what Tom was doing behind me. But I didn't like where this was going.

"What do you mean?" My voice shook.

"You gave up on me, refused to have another go, seven years and I wasn't good enough...but this guy gets a chance?" he seethed.

"You gave up on me Magnus!" I was shouting now. "I wasn't good enough, you gave up on me. I didn't try again, it just happened."

"You expect me to believe that?" he was beyond reason. Magnus had always had a short fuse and when his temper got out of hand there was no arguing with him.

"It's true," Dena came to my defence. "No more IVF, we were all surprised…"

"But it is him, right?" the anger in his eyes wasn't calming. He stared pointedly past me, I could only assume at Tom.

"It's got nothing to do with you," I hissed. I took a step backwards, to move away from him. But I didn't get far. Pain soared up my arm and his big heavy hand wrapped back around my wrist and dragged me back to him roughly.

"Jävla tik! Tell me Ada, har du knulla denna fitta?" He always flipped between languages when he got angry, he lost his head, he forgot himself. But I knew enough Swedish from my years with him, to know he'd just called Tom a 'cunt' and me a 'fucking bitch'.

"Get the fuck off of her," Tom was there again, squeezing himself in front of me and getting up in Magnus' face. He shoved roughly at the taller man's shoulder and I was relieved when I felt the grip on my arm loosen enough for me to pull away. Tom ushered me over in Dena's direction, who grasped my arms in relief and made sure I was well out of the way. But still close enough to see this was far from over.

"I've got to say Adelaide, you've seriously let your standards slip," Magnus was practically snarling, as he and Tom squared up to one another.

"Tom, mate leave it, this isn't your fight," I heard Matt plead, although his face was filled with disbelief, and I knew this wasn't normal behaviour for Tom.

"Yes, it is," Tom didn't tear his eyes from Magnus'.

"So, it's true," Magnus almost grinned, triumphant that Tom

had proved him right. "You're Daddy?"

"You ever fucking lay a hand on Ada again, you ever come near her, or even fucking speak to her –" I didn't hear the rest because Dena's voice caught my attention.

"Ada...is..." I turned to look at my friend, her expression completely unreadable.

"Claudine..." I started, unsure exactly what I could say.

"Don't...just fucking don't," she shook her head and moved away from me. "Matt leave it, come on."

But Matt wasn't listening, he was too busy trying to hold Tom back.

"You'll what?" Magnus taunted him. "Have a right go at me? Try and intimidate me with your fancy words?"

It was Tom who threw the first punch and after that everything was a bit of a blur.

I was tugged out of the way, by who I'm not quite sure. But someone was shouting at me not to get in the way. I could hear Dena above everyone, shouting at Matt, telling him to leave Tom, he didn't deserve his help. Then at Tom, laying into him.

I could hear words like 'After all we've done for you' and 'Lying, cheating, bastard'. I wanted to stop her, to try and explain. But I couldn't. It was like my mouth was glued shut. I was fighting an internal battle, unsure of whose side I should be on, or what I could possibly say to simultaneously calm Dena down and beg her forgiveness, and stop the fist fight which had broken out between my ex-boyfriend and the father of my child.

"Magnus! Stop!" I screamed, eventually finding my voice. Tom might have started the fight, but Magnus was bigger and stronger. I'd seen people end up on the wrong side of Magnus before and the result was not a good one. But Tom was giving as good as he got. Apparently, he could hold his own in a fight and that did surprise me given his slight build. But I winced when Magnus' fist connected with Tom's jaw. Tom staggered to the side and as he did Matt grabbed him by the shoulders.

"That's enough! I suggest everyone gets out right now or I'm calling the police," It was Gerald, the owner of the establishment. He was now standing between both men. He addressed Magnus who was being held back by two of the pubs patrons. "Get out, get a cab and go home Magnus. Sober up and call the lady in the morning to apologise. You're out of line man."

Then he turned to Tom, "And I don't know who the hell you are, but anyone who starts throwing punches in my bar, regardless of the reason, is not welcome back here. Get the fuck out, both of you."

Magnus left first, the two people who had been holding him off Tom, dragged him out of the pub, I hoped to throw him into a taxi. Matt dragged Tom out the front door, Dena in tow and me trailing reluctantly behind. As we hit the fresh air, Matt shoved Tom out of his grip. Tom stumbled slightly and fell against the wall.

"Dena…" I started.

"I don't want to hear it, Ada."

"Please let me at least try and explain."

"No! You've had weeks to explain, but you didn't…your girl-friend was pregnant!" she screamed at Tom, then she turned to me. "You knew, you knew and you still slept with him, and then...you didn't tell me. I thought I knew you, Ada. My Ada wouldn't do that... and she wouldn't lie to me either. I might have gotten over you fucking him..." She pointed at Tom, "But I can't forgive you for lying to me –"

"Dena, it's not what you think, I can explain why –"

"Repeatedly! For months! You were never going to tell me. You're the worst friend and you know what? You're a terrible fucking mother as well," Dena screamed.

"Matt," I choked his name, hoping he might allow me to speak. But of course, he was going to side with his wife. He just shook his head and took Dena's hand. He walked her to the edge of the pavement and hailed down a passing cab.

"Leave it, Ada. Just get yourself home and give her time," Matt sighed, shoving his angry and drunk wife into the taxi.

"I don't need fucking time, I need a new best friend!" Dena shouted past him. I wasn't a crier. I had always been a tough cookie and rarely let my emotions show, but her words tore me to pieces. My eyes burned and I couldn't control the first few tears which escaped and trickled down my cheeks.

"Please Ada, just get in a taxi and go home. Be safe. But I mean it. It's pointless trying to make things right with her now," Matt jumped into the cab and shut the door behind him and it sped off down the deserted street.

I watched the car disappear, as it turned off at the end of the road. I sniffled and took a shaky breath. I knew Matt was right. Dena was drunk and although genuinely hurt, she would not be in any fit state to listen to me until she'd sobered up and calmed down. I peered down the road hoping it wouldn't be long until another cab passed by.

It'd forgotten Tom was still there. I was so distraught, and shell-shocked by the whole ordeal of the evening. I only remembered his presence when I heard a long, pained groan from behind me. I turned to see him, several feet away, sitting against the wall of the pub. His knees were drawn up and his face buried in his hands.

I hesitated. Part of me just wanted to get in the next cab, go home, curl up in bed and cry. But it was Tom. I couldn't leave him like this. Drunk and injured in the middle of London. I quickly brushed my tears away and approached him. I crouched in front of him, just about stopping the groan that escaped me every time I moved in a way my body didn't agree with in my pregnant state.

"Tom," I said his name quietly, reaching out and brushing my fingers over his swollen knuckles. He dropped his hands from his face and looked at me. His poor beat up face. Blood smeared through his beard and down his throat. There was swelling trailing up the left side of his face, from his jaw, to his eye, and I could see a bruise already forming, even under the dim street lights. His glasses were damaged and now sitting at an odd angle on his face, I reached forward and took them off for him, offering a small smile as I did. The look he gave me was one of remorse and guilt. He opened his mouth to say something, but I stopped him. "Come on, let's get you home."

CHAPTER TWELVE

So close, yet so far...

"Is it this key?" I frowned, trying to work out the shapes of all the keys jangling on the bunch I'd managed to get Tom to hand over to me on the taxi ride to his home.

He'd spent the journey mumbling apologies and insisting that he'd never behaved like that in his life and he had no idea what had come over him. He was inconsolable, burying his face into my neck and holding my hands, begging my forgiveness. But that really wasn't my main concern right now.

I was more worried about the slur to his words and whether that was due to the fresh air making the alcohol rush to his head, or possible concussion. I did consider asking the taxi driver to take us to the hospital to at least get Tom checked out. But the second I'd voiced my concern to Tom, he'd shot me down in an instant, assuring me that he was fine and that he just needed to get home and go to bed.

"Silver one," Tom mumbled, reaching out to take the keys from my fingers. He held them close to his face, I guessed because he couldn't see very well without his glasses. "This...it's this one," he held the bunch up by the key in question, looking stupidly proud of himself for his small triumph. I took it from him and turned to unlock the door to the ground floor flat in the converted townhouse, praying that he'd at least remembered which house was his, in his less than sober state.

"Where's Buddy?" I questioned, warily checking as I let us in, not wanting the young dog to escape if he was loose in the flat.

"Sleep in the kitchen," Tom waved a hand, gesturing into the hallway as he followed me inside, tripping up the step as he did and staggering through the doorway. He grabbed onto door-frame to balance himself.

"Woah, careful Tom, mind the steps!"

"Sorry."

"Just...be careful, I can't find the light switch," I felt around the walls in the dark hallway, until my hand landed on the little square plastic box. I flicked the switch, "Ah ha!" The entrance way filled with light and I moved back past Tom to close the front door.

Tom stood watching me silently, whilst I looked around, peering into each room to get my bearings. I stepped inside the kitchen and a sleepy Buddy peered up from his doggy bed. "Hello gorgeous boy, you go back to sleep, I'm going to get your silly Daddy patched up and put to bed."

I hunted through the cupboards until I found a glass and filled it with water. I pushed it into Tom's hands as I passed him again in the hall, where he stood gormlessly. I found the bathroom and looked in the cabinet, "There you are!" I was quite pleased with myself, when I located a little green first aid kit. He was a doctor, of course he kept a fully stocked first aid kit in his house. I peered out into to the hall, "Tom, come here," He walked slowly into the small bathroom and I pointed at the bath, "Just sit on the edge of the bath, I'm going to sort your face out."

"It's fine, I'll do it, I'm a Doctor…"

"Tom, you're drunk."

"You should go home, Ada. You and the baby need to sleep…" He reached his hand out to touch my belly, but I stepped back.

"I'm not going anywhere, Tom, and you'll do as you're told. Now sit down," I told him sternly. Without further argument, he perched himself on the edge of the bathtub.

I found some surgical swabs and a little packet of saline solution. Wetting the swab, I set to work, leaning down to Tom's level and dabbing the drying blood away from his lip and chin. I used a clean flannel from the cupboard to dampen with warm water and wash the excess away from his neck and beard. It didn't look nearly as bad once the blood was cleaned up. His bottom lip was split on the right side and quite swollen. I took out some Arnica cream and applied it to the bruising on his face which had now turned various shades of purple. He hissed as I smoothed some over his temple and jerked away from my touch.

"Stay Still," I admonished.

"Bossy," he mumbled childishly under his breath and I couldn't help but chuckle.

I cleared away the first aid kit, "Right. Shirt off," I instructed, turning back to face him. He stared at me wide eyed. "Tom, take your shirt off. I need to soak it to get the blood out if you ever want to wear it again."

"Course," he nodded quickly looking away and tearing the grey tee shirt with dried blood around the neckline over his head. I averted my eyes, adamant not to look at his body. I should be more cross with him right now. But the only person I was angry with, was myself. I'd been doing my best to block out my current turmoil ever since I'd shoved Tom into the taxi outside the pub. How was I ever going to make things right with Dena?

I took a shaky breath and silently told myself to pull it together, "Okay. You get to bed. I'll bring you another glass of water."

By the time I'd fetched Tom another drink I found him sitting on the edge of his bed. He'd managed to get out of his jeans and into some pyjama bottoms.

"I'm so, so sorry, Ada," he apologised for the hundredth time, as I placed the glass on a bedside table and started yanking the covers on his bed back.

"I know, Tom. Now please get into bed. We can talk tomorrow."

"I won't sleep. Not until I know we are okay," but I knew this was rubbish. He yawned and I had a good idea that as soon as his head hit the pillow he would pass out.

"Tom..." I sighed, standing in front of him, "We are okay. Please can you get into bed."

He nodded, resignedly. But before he moved he looked up at me, "Please can I say good night to him...before you go," I frowned, wondering what he was talking about for a second, until his eyes flicked to my belly.

"Oh...erm," what was the harm, really? "Sure. Go ahead."

I moved a little closer and Tom reached out placing a large hand either side of my bump and leant closer. I wasn't sure what he was going to do. Then I felt to skirt of my dress scrunching in his hands. But I didn't stop him. He moved my dress up and over my belly, revealing my bare legs, and high waisted, lace knickers. And my much bigger stomach. It protruded outwards and already I had a couple of stretch marks around my sides. But Tom was unbothered.

His lips pressed softly to my swollen tummy. He dropped his head lower, trailing butterfly kisses around my belly button. "Good night little man. Daddy loves you," He murmured into my skin. Then he pushed one last kiss to my belly and dropped the fabric of my dress, so I was covered again and without looking at me he crawled into bed and pulled the covers up to his neck. "Thank you, Ada."

"Good night, Tom," I mumbled, holding back another flood of tears.

*

At first, I'd not really been sure what to do. I'd seriously considered letting myself out and going home. But then my concern about Tom's concussion and remembering something about not letting someone fall asleep after a blow to the head, kept me lingering in the hallway outside his bedroom.

I didn't want to be alone either. I wasn't sure that I wanted to be with Tom right now, but it seemed preferable than getting a cab back to an empty flat and wallowing in the depressing aftermath of my own fuck up. My heart started racing and my throat tightened as panic set in, what if she never forgave me? I gasped, sucking in a huge gulp of air, in an attempt to regulate my breathing.

I was staying put. I helped myself to a drink, then looked for the second bedroom. I found it at the end of the hall, a good size single room and there was a bed. But the bed was unmade and covered in boxes, some opened, some not. The rest of the room was crammed with junk that Tom was clearly still sorting through from his recent move.

I sighed and went through to the lounge, which I'd found earlier when looking for the kitchen and bathroom. I dragged off a throw which was folded neatly over the back of the sofa and got myself as comfortable as I could, then I attempted to sleep.

It wouldn't go down in history as the best nights sleep I'd ever had. But I was tired from all the action of the evening and the emotional stress knocked me out quickly. But I was woken early, by Buddy nuzzling my hand and an uncomfortable ache in my lower back. Pregnant women should not sleep on sofas.

It was light outside, but when I peered out the window the street was deserted and I knew it was still ridiculously early. This was confirmed when I checked my phone and the time read ten minutes past six.

I got myself up and stood outside Tom's bedroom door, which I'd not completely shut. I could hear his heavy breathing from inside, telling me he was sleeping soundly and there was no sign of him starting the day anytime soon. So, I pottered on. Cleaning myself up a little in the bathroom, removing my smudged make-up from last night and waking myself up a bit more.

I found Buddy's food and gave him breakfast, which he was extremely grateful for. I checked my phone constantly. I wasn't sure when it would be too early to call Dena, or even if I should call her. Maybe I should just go around there. I was desperately trying to push down the sickening feeling that rose in me, every time I considered the fact that there was a chance she might never talk to me again. I didn't want to get upset and I didn't want Tom to see me upset. He'd blame himself and it was as much my fault as it was his. Tom started the lie, but I'd made the decision to continue it.

By nine o'clock I'd helped myself to some breakfast, tidied the bathroom and put a load of washing on for Tom. I'd also taken Buddy for a little walk down the road, because he'd been hankering at the door and I knew Tom was normally an early riser.

When I finally heard movement from Tom's room, a slight creak of the floorboards and the chain flushing in the ensuite bathroom, I put the kettle on. But Tom didn't come out of his room.

I made a cup of tea and approached the bedroom cautiously. I gently tapped on the door and pushed it open. Tom was in bed, sitting against the headboard, hand cradling the side of his face, looking very surprised to see me.

"You're still here?" His voice was groggy and he dropped his hand to his lap. The bruising on his face had come out more through the night and I knew he must be in a fair bit of pain.

"I told you I wasn't going anywhere," I approached the bed and set the drink down next to him, "I made you some strong tea, I wasn't sure if you normally took sugar, but I put two in, because it helps when you've been drinking."

"Thank you."

"How are you feeling?"

"My heads throbbing and my face hurts."

"Magnus packs one hell of a punch."

144

"You're telling me."

We looked at each other, silence surrounding us for a couple of moments, before I felt the need to break it. "I erm...I fed Buddy and took him for a walk. He's such a good boy."

"You didn't have to do that."

"I did actually, he wouldn't leave me alone," I smirked and Tom shook his head, before wincing at the movement.

"I'm so sorry, Ada. For last night, for starting something with your ex, and for Claudine...I...I should never have asked you to lie to her."

"No, you shouldn't have...but it was my decision to keep lying. I'm not happy with you, I was never happy about being asked to lie. But...we're both to blame. I won't allow you to bear the brunt of it. As for Magnus...I should have told him. He deserved better than to find out like that. He might have...he might have been the one who gave up and ended with me, but I still owed it to him to be the one to tell him. You're an idiot, you shouldn't have hit him," I sighed and turned around, so I could sit on the edge of Tom's bed.

"I know, I'm s –"

"You're sorry, yes, you keep saying," I snapped, "It doesn't matter now anyway. I really couldn't give a shit about Mags, I just... I've fucked up and I've lost my best friend and I have no idea what to do."

"Do you not think she'll forgive you?"

I shook my head, quickly brushing away the few tears that I'd managed to keep away all morning, "I don't think so. She's so stubborn, and I've hurt her in the worst possible way. But what's worse is... and this is so selfish. But all I keep thinking is that I have no one now. I'm going to be on my own. I know I have my Mum and Dad, but... Dena was going to be my birth partner, she was going to stay in my flat after the baby comes to help me at home. I was so lucky to have her. I've ruined everything and now I don't know what I'm going to do. I don't think I can do this...I can't do this."

My shoulders shook as the realisation took over. I was truly alone now. I hadn't been scared before. I had a support network. But I'd destroyed it. I felt Tom's arms around me before I knew what was happening. He was pulling me down next to him and closing me in his hold. I lifted my feet onto the bed and turned into his body, allowing him to hold me. I lay on top of the covers and him still beneath them, but our bodies pressed together. His hand cradled the back of my head, and my face pressed against his bare best.

"You aren't alone, Ada. I promise you. I'm not going to let that happen."

I sniffled and mumbled into his skin, "You need to make up your mind, Tom. I won't let you float in and out of our child's life."

"My heart knew what it wanted the day we found out you were pregnant, Ada. It's just been fighting with my head. But I've known all along there is no way I can stand back and be an absent parent. I already love him," Tom's voice trembled, as he made his admission, "I'm just scared I'm not good enough. I've really, really fucked up and I'm terrified of hurting you, and him."

I pulled back just enough to speak to him properly, but I didn't look at him, "I don't want you to do this out of a sense of obligation. Because you blame yourself for me losing Dena."

"I promise you. Fuck…" He almost growled, "Last night, when he…Magnus grabbed your arm, something came over me. Something so fucking primal, I could have torn his throat out. I'm not a violent man, but seeing him threaten you, hurt you…"

"I'm okay, Tom. He didn't hurt me." I lifted my arm, to show him no damage was done, but he took it gently in his hand, examining it anyway to be sure.

"Please believe me when I say I'm not just having a change of heart because I feel obligated to. Last night, being unable to protect you, protect our baby," Tom's eyes darted down between us, then back up to mine, "I felt so powerless."

"What are you saying?"

"I'm not going anywhere, Ada. I'm here for you, not just for financial support, but whatever kind of support you need. And I'm going to be there for our baby boy. Always."

I craned my head up so I could see him properly. He still held my wrist in his hand, stroking it gently with his thumb and his head rested on the pillow. I tugged my hand from his grip and ran my fingers carefully over his swollen brow. "I'd like that," I said quietly. Tom looked down again so our eyes met and he smiled

I couldn't stop myself. I shuffled up the bed and before Tom could stop me, I'd pressed my lips against his. I didn't care that his breath smelt like stale alcohol and his lips were dry against mine. I just needed him. It only occurred to me when my mouth was on his, that he'd not actually said he wanted me as anything other than the mother of his child. I had no place kissing him. The second I realised this, I jerked backwards, only to feel Tom's grip on my body tighten and just as our kiss broke, his mouth was on mine again. He was kissing me back, but not forcefully. It was slow and lazy, his tongue begged entry, and I allowed it. It was only when a metallic taste filled my mouth, I remembered his split lip.

"Shit, Tom," I yanked away and he looked panicked, like maybe he'd done something terribly wrong, "Your mouth," I cupped his chin with my hand and gingerly touched his lip with my thumb, it was bleeding a little.

"It's okay, it doesn't hurt," He assured me.

"But it's bleeding."

"It doesn't matter, come back here," He practically whined, tugging me back into his body. He pecked my nose, then my chin and trailed a few kisses down my jaw. "See, it's fine." He pressed his lips to mine again. His forehead came to rest against mine, so we could look each other right in the eyes. "Fuck, you drive me crazy, Ada."

"Really?"

"Yes."

"Why didn't you say anything?"

"Have you seen you? You're stunning, a woman like you would never be interested in me. I thought, had you been completely sober, you'd have never slept with me that night. I was really chancing my arm when I suggested it. Despite everything, I felt so, so lucky."

"That's ridiculous, Tom," I couldn't believe what I was hearing, "You were so...confident and in control. No one's ever made me...I mean...I've never had someone who... you made me come twice!"

That made Tom laugh, loudly. I giggled as he finally pulled back a bit and relaxed back onto the pillow. As we parted, a wave of guilt churned in my stomach. What on earth was I doing? I should be leaving his flat right now and going straight to Matt and Dena's. I shouldn't be fooling around with the person who initiated this entire mess. A low groan from Toms lips caught my attention and I looked at him just as his hand flew up to his head. "Fuck... my head."

"I'll get you some paracetamol, I saw some in the kitchen."

"You're not going anywhere," Tom growled, grabbing me before I could get up fully and pulling me back down on the bed next to him. "I'll be fine, as long as you don't go anywhere."

I giggled, "Well if you are going to keep me in bed with you, until you've rested off your hangover, then I'm getting comfortable," I started scrambling to get under the covers, but Tom stopped me.

"You'll crease your dress."

"Tom, I slept in it, it's already creased," I rolled my eyes.

"Well, you'll get hot, I think you should take it off."

"Oh, you do, do you?" I smirked, kneeling up on the bed next to him.

"No funny business, I promise. I just think you'll be more comfortable, I'm looking out for your best interests."

I snorted, and Tom quirked an eyebrow. "I think I'll keep it on."

"Take the dress off, Ada," *Fuck.* That tone meant business. The firm, no nonsense timbre in his voice gave me an instant flash-back, to all those months ago when he ordered me to keep my arms above my head. Verbally restraining me. Once again, I knew I was going to do exactly what he told me. I obediently lifted my dress by it's hem and tugged it over my head, then tossed it across the room. "Better?"

"Much," His eyes raked my body, lingering longer on my stomach, but also appreciating my lace clad breasts, which were practically fighting their confines. I already needed another new bra. Tom lifted the covers, so I could get under and I immediately snuggled up next to him. It was an odd feeling, I hardly knew this man. But suddenly, I was surrounded by him, his body, his belongings and his overwhelming natural scent, and I'd never felt more secure in my entire life.

"I can't stay all day," I told him, just after he sweetly kissed my lips again, "I need to go to Dena's, see if I can get her to talk to me."

"I should come with you."

"I think it would be better if you didn't," he nodded and kissed me again, a bit harder this time. When he turned his body completely into mine, I let my hand run up his back and neck, and my fingers combed through his hair, tangling into his auburn curls and tugging gently. His reaction was primal, one of his hands gripped my backside roughly and his hips bucked against me.

"Ada," he released my name in a breathless groan and attempted to grind his hips into mine, but my larger belly meant we didn't fit together quite so well. So instead his hand left my bum and moved to a breast, cupping briefly, before tugging the material down. My newly enhanced bust didn't need much encouragement to fall from it's confines.

"Tom!" I squeaked, when his head ducked and with no warning, he sucked a nipple into his mouth. "Stop!" He pulled back immediately, looking up at me with concern. "They...are just really, really sensitive," he nodded, understanding, and gently touched a finger to the hardened nub. "Just...uh, be gentle, please."

Nodding, he leant forward, placing a kiss on the tip, then moving back up to my mouth. We kissed for a while longer and things slowly began heating up again. But my heart wasn't in it. I wanted it, I really, really wanted it. But...Dena.

Then, I could hear my phone ringing from the next room. I pulled away and started untangling myself from Tom's arms.

"Leave it."

"I can't. It might be Dena."

Tom didn't argue, when I got up, adjusted my underwear, and left his bedroom in search of my phone. It stopped ringing just as I found it.

"Was it?" Tom asked, when I came back into his room, staring at the screen of my phone.

I shook my head, "No...it was Magnus. He's just text too, he wants to talk to me."

"Ah," Tom collapsed back onto the bed, from where he'd been leaning up on one elbow, and he closed his eyes. He released a long breath, "You should call him back."

CHAPTER THIRTEEN

Alone, Together

I knew something was up when I approached Matt and Dena's house. A van was parked up on the curb and I could read the company lettering 'A J Cooper and Son – Locksmiths' – Fuck. I hurried towards the front door.

"Excuse me?" I asked the man working in the doorway. He looked to be removing the whole lock mechanism from the door.

"Morning love," the man nodded.

"Are they in?" I nodded into the house, but I couldn't get by. I was answered when Matt appeared in the doorway. "What's going on?"

"You need to go, Ada."

"Where is Dena?"

"She doesn't want to see you. She called the locksmith first thing, before I could stop her," He explained. He looked exhausted and I just knew he'd probably had just as little sleep as me. Dena had likely kept him up all night ranting.

"I'd have just given the key back," My chest felt tight, and tears were streaming down my cheeks before I could stop them.

"I told her that...listen... Dena's got every right to be angry with you, fucking hell, Ada, I'm furious with you, and with Tom. But what's worse is that you continued to lie. Both of you, under our roof...he was in a relationship, Ada," Matt shook his head, I could see the disappointment in his eyes.

"But... he wasn't happy. We were drunk, and it just...it just happened. You don't understand, she told him to go elsewhere, so –"

"And you think that makes it alright? Tom may be intelligent, but he's also incredibly stupid sometimes. He shouldn't have stayed with her when she found out she was pregnant by another man. That was his burden to bare. Not yours."

"I know but... I didn't realise this would happen."

"But it did happen and you didn't trust Dena enough to tell her."

"I do trust her, this has nothing to do with trust, Matt. Tom was never going to have an active role in the baby's life, so I thought it was better if no one knew –"

"You're both as stupid as each other," Matt shook his head. "Just go, Ada. If she changes her mind, she'll call you. But don't count on it. You've really gone and blown it."

*

I'd said goodbye to Tom earlier in the day. I'd stayed at his flat long enough to have him sit next to me and hold my hand whilst I had an awkward telephone conversation with Magnus. I apologised for not telling him about the baby. I'd cried when I told him he'd hurt me when he'd grabbed my arm and he apologised for fighting with Tom, who he understood was defending my honour and protecting his child. He said he'd deserved the punch in the face, and even said he would have done the same, had it been his baby I was carrying. That had made me cry even more.

Tom kissed me on the cheek and when I left he had told me he was going to shower and likely head back to bed to sleep off the remainder of his hangover. I promised to call him after I'd seen Dena, to let him know how it had gone. He wanted to speak to Matt but we agreed it was better for me speak to them both first.

Now I found myself back on Tom's doorstep. Uncontrollable tears poured from my eyes and I shivered, even though it was mid-September and not at all cold. He only lived two roads down from Dena and Matt and after being told to sling my hook, I'd not known where else to turn.

She'd changed the fucking locks. That's how much she hated me.

It felt like I'd been waiting a lifetime when Tom finally answered the door and I flung myself at him, clinging onto him and sobbing hysterically. God only knows what he must have thought of me. But he didn't speak, simply closed the door and allowed me to continue crying into his tee shirt.

He remained still long enough for my distraught blubbering to calm to a steady sniffling, then he gently urged me through his flat and into his living room, where he carefully deposited me onto the sofa.

I drew my knees up and buried my face in my hands straight

away and a fresh wave of bawling overtook me. I truly don't think I'd ever cried so much in my life, or ever felt so bereft, or heartbroken. I had shed tears when Magnus had ended out relationship. Private ones, where I wept at the wasted memories that we'd made together. When our first round of IVF failed, I had been sad, and disappointed, but I'd held my head high and said, 'maybe next time'. Magnus and I had shared some tears together.

But now, I felt complete and utter devastation.

I was vaguely aware of the sofa dipping next to me and I jerked when Tom's hand touched my leg, unable to reach me anywhere else. "Is there anything I can do?" I didn't have to tell him what the matter was. He already knew. I just shook my head into my hands. So, Tom just sat with me, occasionally brushing a hand over my knee, or leaning to stroke my hair. He made small comforting gestures, whilst I shuddered and hiccoughed. Embarrassingly, every once in a while a pained whimper would travel up through my chest and out through my lips. The baby was doing somersaults, probably wondering what the hell all the noise was about.

I wasn't sure how much time had passed when I felt Tom get up. He didn't say anything he just left the room. Seconds later I heard him speaking from somewhere else in the flat. His voice was muffled and I was sure he'd shut himself in a different room so I couldn't hear. But I could just about make snippets of his end of the conversation.

'I know you don't want to talk to me...'

'She's distraught, she knows she's made a mistake but...'

'If Dena was her friend she would at least hear her out.'

'That's cruel and below the belt...'

'She's pregnant, she doesn't need this right now...'

'I'm sorry, Matt...I do appreciate everything, but...'

'If that's how you feel, I understand.'

A door opened and closed and then some clattering sounded from the kitchen. I sat myself up properly and wiped my eyes on the backs of my hands. I was a mess.

An obviously concerned Buddy trotted into the room and sat at my feet for a few minutes. He tilted his head and his big brown eyes were wide with a worry he didn't understand. Then he jumped onto the seat next to me and lay down resting his soft head on my lap. I was playing with his silky ears, and releasing the occasional quiet hiccough when Tom re-entered the room.

He was carrying a plate and a mug which he set down quietly on the coffee table in front of me. I looked up and him and he frowned at Buddy but didn't comment. Of course, he probably didn't allow him on the sofa under normal circumstances.

Tom spoke first, "Tea, two sugars. I've also made you a sandwich because I don't think you've eaten yet today and you need to eat for the baby."

I leant forward and peeling back the bread. Several pieces of thickly sliced cheese lay inside on some heavily buttered white bread.

"You made me a cheese sandwich," I mumbled quietly. Had he remembered? He was quite drunk.

"Yes."

I managed a small smile, showing my gratitude at the gesture and leant forward to bring the plate onto my lap. Tom left my again, so I could eat in piece. It would have been weird for him to sit and watch me. When he came back a little while later he was dressed in dark jeans and a black tee shirt and open hoodie. It only occurred to me then that he'd still been in his pyjama bottoms and a ratty old top when he'd answered the door. He held a dog lead folded up in his hand.

"I'm going to take Buddy for a walk. Would you like to come?"

Buddy's ears pricked up at the word 'walk' but he didn't move. Instead he nuzzled further into my lap and licked my hand. His wet nose pushed up against my belly. It's funny how dogs have a strong sense when something isn't right. He knew I was upset and not even the suggestion of a walk would move him from providing me comfort the only way he knew how.

Fresh air would probably do me good though and I think Tom didn't really know what else to do with me. He was really rather sweet, the way he hung back, being cautious not to overcrowd me. I could tell he wanted to ask a million questions, but he didn't. He held his tongue.

I sniffled and nodded, "Yeah," My voice came out as a husky, croak, "Just let me finish my tea and I'll freshen up first if that's okay?"

"Yep."

"Go on, gorgeous boy, we're going for a walk," With my permission Buddy leapt back to the ground, but he stayed close by. So, concerned was he, that when I opened the bathroom door after splashing my face with water and trying to make it look like I hadn't just spent the best part of an hour crying, I almost tripped right over him.

Lauren Hope

"Buddy!" Tom scalded.

"He's okay."

"You nearly fell right over him."

"But I didn't. He's just worried, he's very sweet."

We walked in silence to the park. Buddy trotted along in front of us, peering back every now and again to check on me. I groaned when I realised Tom had lead us to the entrance to Primrose Hill. A walk was one thing, I hadn't signed up for a work out.

"Everything okay?"

I nodded, "It's fine," I lied.

Tom obviously didn't believe me, but we continued walking. A few minutes later Tom finally piped up, "I'm travelling to my Mum's tonight."

"Oh," I didn't mean to sound so surprised. Of course, he had plans for the weekend, he had a life that didn't just revolve around work and getting random women knocked up at weddings.

"I just thought you should know...I don't have to go, I can stay if you need me to –"

"What? Why would I need you too?"

"Well, you're very upset, I wouldn't want to leave you...I'm worried about you."

"Don't be silly, I wouldn't expect you to change your plans for me. You've been great, I'm sorry for barging in on you like that, I wasn't really sure where else to go."

"I'm glad you came to me."

"What are you going to tell your Mum? About your face?" I gestured to his battered jaw and brow. To be honest, now in the daylight it wasn't quite so bad. Surprisingly the bruising had already faded from its harsh reds and purples, to paler purples and blues.

"Well, the truth probably," I nodded and looked back to the path, then he spoke again, "I'm going to tell her about the baby."

"Really?"

"Well yes, things have changed now, Ada. My family need to know," He explained, "I mean, she'll be upset...not because of the baby," He added the last bit as an afterthought, maybe seeing my suddenly concerned expression. "I've made some really awful mistakes this past year. My family... well they weren't exactly pleased by my decision to raise another man's baby. They didn't understand. But...Mum eventually came around to the idea. She was getting excited about being a Granny again. When it all fell apart...well she was quite heartbroken and the rest of the family basically said, 'I told you so'."

"But he is your baby, it's different isn't it?"

"Yes, it is. But the circumstances are... well my Mum and Dad will be very disappointed in my behaviour. Mum will cry and Dad will tell me I'm old enough to know better...which I am."

"Takes two to tango, if they're cross with you, they're going to hate me."

"My Mum's never hated anyone."

"I could be the exception," I shrugged. But his news that he planned to tell his family about the baby, made me realise that I had to explaining to do, to my own. "Perhaps I should go home for a few days."

"Home?"

"Brighton."

"Ah. Will you erm...tell them about me?" Tom looked a little uncertain of his question.

"Listen, Tom..." I took a shaky breath, I knew what I was about to say could completely ruin everything. Today had already been a difficult day, "About this morning. I think...maybe we got a bit carried away and it was good it stopped when it did."

I stopped walking. We were only half way up the hill, and it wasn't the steepest incline, but I was already getting a stitch in my side and a dull ache in my lower back. "Do you need to sit down?" Tom asked gently, seeing me reach to put a hand on my back, and groan a little. There was a bench on the footpath just a few feet away. I didn't want to give up, but perhaps this conversation was better had sitting down. So, I nodded.

Tom gently, and cautiously took my elbow and lead me to sit down. When he sat next to me, he looked to be mentally preparing himself for my complete rejection, and I felt awful. I shouldn't have just come out with it like that, "I do want you!" Okay, so maybe it shouldn't have come out like that either.

"Erm –"

"What I mean is...well we don't actually know each other that well. I'm really hormonal at the moment and I don't want to jump into bed with you just because I'm basically turned on ninety percent of the time. I don't want us to hurt each other, if we carry on like this, and then in a few months' time we realise we don't really like each other that much, and things get awkward. Then we end up arguing over custody and hating each other's guts."

Tom was nodding, slowly, taking in everything I had just said, "I agree."

"I'm sorry…"

"No…" Tom reached up and ran a hand through his hair, "I mean, you are completely right, we should be focusing on the baby. But us getting along is a really important part of that. That said, I don't think my feelings toward you will change…"

"Can we date?"

Tom smiled, the first proper, genuine smile I'd seen from him all day, "We can date."

I stood to start walking again, and Tom joined me as we continued uphill. I side eyed him a few times and couldn't help but grin to myself at how positively delighted he looked. "You know… as we are dating and all, you can hold my hand if you like. That's allowed, I'd like it if you did."

Tom didn't answer, but instead he swapped Buddy's lead to his other hand and reached for mine. He laced our fingers together and gave it a gentle squeeze. Our joined hands relaxed to a light swing between us as we continued to the top of the hill.

*

I arrived in Brighton quite late on the Saturday night. I only told my Mum I was visiting once I was on the train. She was, understandably worried by my unexpected visit.

Dad met me at the station and drove me back to their home. No questions were asked, and I'd gone straight to bed, utterly exhausted from my eventful day.

My parents lived just on the edge of the city, in the affluent area of Roedean. When I was little, their home was in some luxurious apartments right on the beachfront in the city centre, right in the middle of the action. That's where Mum liked it in her younger days. These days she preferred the quieter life and the outdoor heated pool.

My parents were, to put in in no nicer context, loaded. Although, other than their beautiful five-bedroom home overlooking the English Channel, they didn't really act it. When I was at school, I used to think my family painfully normal in comparison to my friend's families. I was fortunate to receive a good, private education, but I made my own choices and had always supported myself. I was taught to look after my money and never take anything for granted.

More important than money was love, and my family had that in scores. My Mum was unconventional and a little crazy. She's overbearing, but it all comes from her heart. She identifies as Pagan these days, but that's a recent spiritual discovery. She was raised in a devout catholic home, and hated the rules imposed upon her by her own family. She had disowned them the moment she was old enough and ended up travelling the world and 'finding herself'. She considered herself some sort of medium, and claimed to be able to read palms, and auras. I adore my Mum, but bless her, she's never once made any accurate predictions concerning my own life.

My Dad adores my Mum. I think that's the only reason he puts up with her crazy ways. They do have their own interests and for the most part lead quite separate lives. My Dad will forever have music in his veins and still spends most of his free time at a variety of life music events. Everything from rock festivals to the opera. But as he's got older, he's also taken a keen interest in Golf.

But almost forty years of marriage spoke volumes about the love they had for one another.

For late September, it was still quite warm on the south coast. A calm breeze blew in, but it was temperate enough for me to enjoy an early morning swim when I got up the next day. I was sitting on the edge of the pool, enjoying the view and unconsciously smoothing my hand over my bump when my Mum interrupted my thoughts.

"You look pretty today, my love," my Mum always said that, almost every day that she saw me.

"So, do you, Mum," I smirked up at her, then I screwed up my face, "I'm really not in the mood for Yoga this morning...or at all, ever again."

"Me neither," she pulled up the skirts of her floaty maxi dress and joined me on the edge of the pool. "Talk to me lovely, tell me what the matter is, I'm so worried."

"I...I've fallen out with Dena."

"Oh...gods..." Mum's voice was breathless. Dena and I had never fallen out before, and she knew that.

"I lied to her, I…it's my fault. I… she won't talk to me, won't allow me to explain, she hates me," I shuddered, suddenly feeling a chill in the air that wasn't there before. I turned to look at my Mum, taking in her stricken expression, her pale face surrounded by a storm of fiery red hair. That was natural, at fifty-eight years old she was lucky not to have one single streak of grey. I'd not inherited her red curls, but instead, naturally my Dad's thick, dark blonde waves. Which I crucified with bleach and ridiculous colours. I suddenly thought of Tom, with his almost red curls, and wondered if our little boy would inherit a head of ginger curls. My heart almost skipped a beat at this lovely thought.

So, I started telling Mum all about Tom. About our stupid one-night stand, not all the gory details obviously. But the events leading up to it and what happened after. About Grace, about how she'd treated Tom, which, I'd decided was really, quite appallingly. Tom had his faults and he'd made mistakes but… he was going to raise her child. He wanted to love her, and she simply wouldn't let him. She permitted him to go elsewhere for affection and intimacy, then punished him when he did. She left him with a world of insecurities, when all he'd done was try and support the woman he loved.

I told Mum how I'd withheld the truth from Dena, but not only that, continued to lie, with Tom right under her roof. I gave my reasons for doing so, my own defence, but I also acknowledged my mistakes. I told her about Magnus, and the encounter in the pub. Also, about our conversation yesterday morning in which he was apologetic and understanding.

"Magnus was a fool for letting you go, and he knows it," were my Mum's first words, "But I also think, Dena is being a bit harsh, and very Dena in her dramatics. I do think she might calm down."

"She changed the fucking locks!"

"We all do impulsive things when we are angry."

"I don't blame her for being angry."

"And you shouldn't. But she can't stay angry forever. She will eventually calm down and maybe then she will allow you explain to her, and to apologise properly. Then it's up to her to decide if she wishes to forgive you. But…twelve years of friendship is a lot to throw away," Mum reached over and lay a hand on top of mine, the one which still rested on my belly

"He's asleep. I think the swim calmed him. He's been wreaking havoc in there for the past two days," I nodded down to my bump. "I'm sorry Mum, I should have told you too."

"You didn't lie to me. You told me you'd had a one-night stand, you told me the father didn't want to be involved, but would support you financially," She looked at me, intensely, "That's still true isn't it?"

"Yes…well…I mean, that is all true but…Tom has had a change of heart," my Mum's eyes softened.

"You light up when you speak about him."

"I can't wait to meet him," I looked down and stroked my belly again.

"No, I mean Tom. He's special to you, isn't he? I can see it you know, in your aura. It's conflicted, I can see your sadness and pain. It's there, all around you…but there is also a calm, a happiness…"

"Mum…" I warned, narrowing my eyes.

"Tell me about him."

"He's…tall-ish and slim. He has curly hair, and he wears glasses, he's a bit older, he's a Cardiologist. He has a lovely puppy called Buddy –"

"I didn't ask what he looked like, Ada. You know that," Mum was very straight up. She wanted me to be honest, and I had to be now. I'd lied enough.

"He's kind and thoughtful. Refined, he's not a loud man, although the fact that he started a fight with Mags"'9, would make you believe otherwise. He's sweet, funny, and sometimes a little awkward, especially if he thinks he's offended you, then he apologises constantly. But he's also confident, and in control and –"

"And you like him," she cut me off, and she was smiling at me.

"Yes."

"Does he like you?"

"I think he's a little in awe of me, and sometimes intimidated by me. But he tries not to show it. We're spending more time together, getting to know each other. It's important we get along, for the baby," that was what we'd agreed to tell our families. It was why I'd told Tom I didn't think jumping into bed together was the best idea just yet. When he asked if I was going to tell them about him, I needed to clarify what I was saying. Also, what he was allowed to tell his family about me.

"I think that's sensible," Mum agreed, "Now you just have to tell your Dad, and you'd better call your brother."

CHAPTER FOURTEEN

A new kind of life

Twenty-Seven Weeks

It had been three weeks since I'd last seen or spoken to Dena. She'd deleted me from any form of social media. I'd cried when I realised. I wasn't much of a social media fan, not like she was. She was the selfie queen. Which I think is why it hurt so much. Because it didn't mean much to me, but it held a much higher importance to her.

I had tried. I'd tried calling her multiple times. Each time the line just cut off after several rings. Then one day I tried, and the number would not connect. Then I called Matt. He did answer – he told me I needed to stop trying to contact Dena. So, I did.

Very suddenly it was like her entire existence had been removed from my life. All I had were the photos adorning the walls of my little flat. They hurt so much to look at, but I didn't have the heart to take them down.

Tom had been amazing.

My coping strategy had been to bury myself in my work. I'd ended up staying at my parent's house for nearly a week. The weather had been so nice and both of them had been so supportive. They didn't judge or berate me for my actions. Instead they simply listened when I wanted to talk and gave me space when I didn't. Which made a change, not so much for my Dad, but Mum had always liked to interfere.

I enjoyed the peace and quiet away from the city, but I knew I had to return eventually. Tom had kept in near constant contact whilst I was away. He thought it was good that I was having a break, but I could tell he was desperate to see me again. We spoke a lot on the phone and he'd told me all about his family's reaction to the news.

As predicted his Mum had cried. She'd been unable to speak to him for several hours as the news sunk in. But when she did, she asked him a lot of questions, mostly about me. But also, about his involvement and how much she would be able to be involved. By the time he left, she'd started to come around to the idea. She'd even asked if she could meet me, although Tom had thankfully put her off, at least for now.

His Dad had not taken the news quite so well. He'd had to break it to him over the phone, as he lived in Cumbria these days on the outskirts of Carlisle and Tom rarely saw him in person, he'd told me at most three or four times a year. He was bitterly disappointed and made it abundantly clear to Tom that whatever Tom's decision was he wanted no part in it. I felt horrid about this, although Tom kept assuring me that it was no great loss, not to him, or the baby, and certainly not to me. He didn't say as much but I got the distinct feeling he and his Dad had always had a somewhat fractious relationship.

The one thing he didn't seem open to discussing was the state of his friendship with Matt. I'd tried to ask him a few times, but each time I broached the subject he would swiftly divert the conversation. I wasn't sure if that was for my benefit or his. But Tom was positive, at least on the outside.

So, when I got home and resigned to spending my days engrossed in editing tracks, and creating new mixes, some for work, some for myself, Tom took it upon himself to turn up with food and pull me back to the real world. Or phone me in the middle to the day to make sure I'd got up and showered. He encouraged me to leave the flat to get fresh air, by inviting me on early morning or even late evening walks with him and Buddy.

We'd spent the last two weekends together. Mostly at his place, but I never stayed. It was too soon for that. We also went out, Tom liked to treat me. Dinners in nice restaurants, walks in the park. The Cinema and the theatre. He always had a surprise up his sleeve and I'd never really experienced that sort of treatment in a relationship. He was spontaneous and although I wanted to tell him he didn't need to try and impress me with romantic gestures, but I didn't want them to stop either, because I was enjoying being spoilt, possibly for the first time in my life. I was also grateful for the distraction, because when I was with Tom, I wasn't thinking about Dena.

"I've got you something," Tom announced, as I let him into my little flat. I'd been working almost constantly, and he was early. I was still in my tatty house clothes, with my headphones hanging around my neck and my face bare of make-up. It was nothing he hadn't seen before, but now we were dating, I was conscious of putting in the extra effort for him.

"You're early."

"Hello to you as well, are we a little grumpy today?" Tom

teased, as he set a thick carrier bag on the table.

"No, I just...look like shit and you look like you," I gestured to his smart navy trousers and ironed white shirt.

"These are my work clothes, those are yours," He shrugged, "You look great, as always, Darling."

"Liar...now give me my present," we were always like this. The banter was nice, it was fun and easy.

Tom reached into the bag and pulled out a box shaped object and handed it to me. It was weighty and I worked out it was books. Children's books, 'Winnie the Pooh' to be precise, in a lovely little collection box. "Erm...thanks?"

"Well, they are more for the baby really. I passed the bookshop and they were in the window and I just... I loved those books when I was little."

"Me too," I nodded, and smirked up at him, "But you do know, despite having two incredibly smart parents, verging on genius, the baby can't read yet."

"You're hilarious," Tom said, deadpan. "I actually thought, we could read to him. You know, whilst he's in there," Tom pointed to my belly.

I laughed. Then I saw the serious expression on Tom's face, his much more attractive face, now the bruising had completely gone, and his lip completely healed. He'd also got his glasses fixed and no longer lived in contact lenses. I really liked him in his glasses, "Oh, erm...you're serious."

"Well, not if you don't want to," I'd offended him.

"No, no, Tom, sorry, I'm sorry. I just..." I set the books down on my table and walked up to him. I reached up, so I could hang my arms around his neck and tiptoed so I could push a chaste kiss to his lips, "It's a really sweet idea, thank you."

We'd not kissed yet. Not since that morning. Tom had been a complete gentleman. We held hands, he would always greet me with a hug, and give me a peck me on the cheek when we parted. We'd even snuggled once or twice. Usually when he wanted to put his hands on my belly and he always asked my permission first. I'd told him we needed to take it slow, to work out if this was what we both really wanted, and he put the ball completely in my court. I knew he wouldn't make a move until I let him know it was okay.

But the peck on the lips took him by surprise and he stumbled back slightly when I let go of him. Hell, it took me by surprise. I think I'd planned to kiss his cheek, give him a reassuring hug to let him know that I genuinely thought his gesture sweet. But once I was there, his mouth just looked inviting and it felt almost natural to touch my lips to his.

"I've made pasta bake. Do you want to stick it in the oven? I'll go and get changed," I started towards my room, but Tom was hot on my heels.

"Don't get changed, you're comfortable, and you look lovely," I scrunched up my nose.

"I don't feel lovely."

"Ada, you always look gorgeous. I don't think you quite understand how...desirable I find you, all the time. It doesn't matter what you wear," He didn't need to convince me that he was speaking the truth, the desire in his eyes told me exactly what he saw when he looked at me. But it wasn't about him, it was about me and how I felt.

"Well, you wouldn't find me so desirable if you saw what was underneath. I'm wearing an ugly as fuck maternity bra that does nothing more than make me look like I've just got one ginormous boob, not to mention the stretchmarks on my thighs –"

"Ada, do shut up," Tom approached my quickly, quicker than I was prepared for, so when he cupped the back of my head and pressed his mouth hard against mine, it took my breath away. I moaned into the kiss, not realising how much I'd needed it. I needed him so, fucking, much. When he pulled away, his eyes searched mine. They looked different now, his pupils were blown, and they were dark with...lust? "You need to stop talking about what's under your clothes, darling, because right now I want to rip them off, do you understand?"

A small nod, and he let go of me. I whimpered as he did, already missing his touch. But this was for the best, we'd agreed to hold off. It was still only three weeks that we'd been officially dating. I was scared sex might ruin the good thing we had going on.

"What do you think about Jett?" I asked as I was shoving the dirty dinner things into the dishwasher.

"What about it?"

"As a name...for the baby."

"Jett?"

"Yes."

"No."

"Oh?"

"Well, it's not really my decision, but I'd ask you kindly not to make a laughing stock out of my son by burdening him with a name like Jett," I frowned, I thought Jett was cool, a bit offbeat, just like me.

"Fine," I shrugged. "Do you have any suggestions?"

"It's not my decision, Ada, I've not...well I have just spent the best part of three months trying not to consider names," that struck me as very sad. He'd not allowed himself to think about our baby, what he should be called, how he might look?

"It's our decision, Tom. I'd never call our baby a name you didn't like...so Jett is off the table, unless I convince you otherwise."

"You won't," Tom smirked and reached for my wrist, tugging me into him. This affection thing was growing on me. We'd apparently reached a new stage in our relationship. He kissed the top of my head, "We should each make a list."

"Huh?"

"Of names we like. We'll make a list, over the next few weeks, then when we can't think of anymore to add, we'll sit together, and narrow them down. To ones we both like."

"That's a really good idea," I tilted my head up, and we kissed again.

"Hmm, come on, let's sit down, I want to read to my son," I looked at my little two-seater sofa.

"Would it be easier to lie down? More comfortable? We can lie on my bed," I gestured back to my bedroom.

"Ahh…" Tom hesitated, "Well, I'm not sure why you'd think me reading to him, would be easier lying down, the sofa is fine."

"Well, I can think of certain, acoustical advantages which would be easier if we were able to lie down, and spread out," Tom snorted at that, and then laughed.

"Acoustical advantages?"

"Well yes, you can lie near my belly, so he can hear you better."

More laughing, "Sorry, my minds in the gutter."

We did eventually settle on my bed. I lay with my head propped up on some pillows, and Tom lay on his stomach, his head level with my rounded belly. I rolled my top up enough to expose my bump. I knew it wasn't necessary, but it pleased Tom. He asked first and awaited my permission, before pushing a light kiss to my swollen tummy and then laying one large hand over it. With the book open on the bed in front of him, he began to read.

Tom had the most beautiful, low timbre to his voice when he read aloud. It was so relaxing to listen to, I was almost lulled asleep. the only thing keeping me up, was my little baby's constant movements. It felt like he was rolling around in there. He was always most active in the evenings, but I wondered if his current excitement was due to hearing his Daddy's voice so clearly. It certainly made my heart race.

'It's a very funny thought that, if Bears were Bees.

They'd build their nests at the bottom of trees.

And if that being so (if the Bee's were Bears)

We shouldn't have to climb up all these stairs,'

"Oh!" I jumped, opening my eyes, and pushing up on my elbows to see what was wrong. Tom had exclaimed suddenly and stopped reading. He was simply staring at my stomach.

"What's wrong?"

"Was that...did you feel...I...think the baby just moved?"

"You felt it?" I brought a hand down to rest over my tummy, he had been having a little party in there this evening, but I'd not felt him move on the outside yet.

"I think so, is he moving now?" I frowned, quieting for a second so I could concentrate, then I took Tom's hand to where I assumed it was the baby's feet were kicking hard at the inside of my belly.

"He's there," We both were quiet for several long minutes and I continued to feel the usual rolling feeling, and light pressure of my little man inside me. Then suddenly he gave an almighty wallop, and I emitted a squeak.

At the exact same moment Tom took in a gasp of air and looked up at me with a big grin, "That was him, wasn't it, I felt that," I nodded, grinning back at him, delighting in his joy at feeling our baby move for the first time. Tom stayed where he was, splaying both hands over my belly, and we waited to see if he would move again. He did, a few times. Just tiny kicks and punches. "This is the most incredible thing."

"You never felt the baby move with Grace?" I wasn't sure why I asked, part of me wanted to know how much of this experience was a first for Tom.

"Never, she rarely let me touch her," He crawled up the bed and lay next to me, and stroked my hair out of my face, "This is all new to me, Ada."

"Sorry, I don't know why I asked," I suddenly felt bad, this was supposed to be a happy moment and I'd gone and brought up painful memories.

"It's alright, I don't mind you asking questions," He leant forward and kissed me, his lips softly caressing mine. I hummed against his mouth, enjoying the intimacy. I turned my body into his, and pushed myself against him, only spurring on his attack.

My top, which was already pushed up my body, was quickly worked up even further and I sat up to allow Tom to yank it over my head. My ugly maternity bra was forgotten the second Tom's mouth descended onto my neck and travelled down my shoulder in a series of nips and licks.

"Are you sure?" Tom's words were mumbled into my flesh.

"Mmm."

"That's not an answer," Tom stopped his ministrations and lifted his head to look me in the eye. "I don't want to get carried away."

"I don't...I'm not..." I stuttered the words out, right now all I could think about was getting Tom naked and getting him inside me. I was so, so turned on, and my body had been craving the more carnal pleasures for months and I'd been unable to provide it with such. "I really, really need this, Tom, so much that it hurts."

"Is that you talking or your hormones?"

"Does it make a difference?"

"Well... I did promise to help and support you in any way you needed."

"And I need this."

"You do."

"I need you to fuck me, I need to feel you inside me."

"You have such a dirty mouth, Ada."

"What are you going to do about it."

"Well if you weren't pregnant, I'd be taking you over my knee," I balked at that, and I was shocked by the sudden surge of wetness between my thighs. Christ, why was that thought so damn hot?

"You'll just have to find a different way to punish me."

"Indeed, I will...how do I get this thing off?" I realised Tom had been fumbling one handed with the thick backstrap of my monstrous contraption, trying to unclasp it.

"Oh, it's got like a billion hook and eyes..." I sat up and reached back, taking my time to undo it, "Sorry...mood killer."

"It's not that bad, it's got a pretty bow on it," Tom touched the little silk bow in the cleavage of the bra. The manufactures vague attempt to make an otherwise ugly piece of underwear, slightly easier on the eye. I rolled my eyes and tugged it off, slinging it across the room, and it landed over my new collection of furniture against the far wall.

Tom's eyes were immediately on my chest. He dove in, but instead of the sucks and scraping of teeth I was expecting, he began lavishing my nipples with licks and light kisses, whilst his hands groped as much of the flesh as he could hold. He remembered how sensitive I was.

The light touches were all it took to have me writhing beneath him, begging him to hurry up and fuck me. But he was clearly in no rush. As his kisses moved between my breasts, down my abdomen, and over the pregnant swell of my belly, his hair fell over his face, tickling me as he made his journey south. He stopped his journey at the hem of the leggings I still wore.

He paused long enough to stand up, unbutton and remove his own shirt, and hastily divest himself of his trousers and underwear, but not his socks. He was already rock hard, and my mouth watered at the sight. He must have realised I was staring.

"Ada, eyes up here," His voice was firm as he knelt back down on the bed, and I obediently moved my gaze to his face. His eyes searched mine for a second, working me out. I knew why when next words left his lips. He was gauging how I might react to his demand, "I've been wondering for a long time what that pretty, but filthy mouth might feel like around my cock. May I find out, darling?"

I almost pounced him. Moving so quickly he had to stop me with two hands firmly on my upper arms, so I couldn't pin him back on the bed. "Tom," I whined his name, drawing out the 'o' and the 'm'.

"Not on the bed, Ada. I'd love nothing more that to see you on your knees..." He trailed off, and looked down, one hand dropping from my arm, to my belly, and stroking my bump with the tips of his fingers, "If you're able?"

I nodded, unable to refuse him any request. A request no man had ever made of me before, and I had no idea how hot I'd find that suggestion, until I was presented with it. So, I slipped off the bed, sinking to the carpet, and Tom grabbed a pillow, putting it on the floor in front of him and spreading his knees so I could position myself comfortably in between.

I glanced up at Tom, and he gave me a smile of encouragement. I wondered briefly, as I looked back down and tentatively wrapped my hand around his length, if he was always like this in the bedroom? I had no complaints, but I was stunned by his change in demeanour each time things heated up between us. Tom most definitely had a kink for control in the bedroom, I'd learnt that the first, and so far, only time we'd slept together. I could only speculate how far that kink might go?

I licked the bead of precum which had gathered and was glistening at the head of Tom's cock, then closed my mouth around the tip.

A low groan, and then a whispered curse left Tom's lips above me. I set to work, I'd always been able to give good head. Possibly not something I should be too proud of, or admit to openly, but feedback (albeit mostly from one man) told me that I had a natural skill. The heavy breathing and muttered words of praise from Tom, strengthened the truth behind this. I dipped my head, at a steady pace, taking in a little more each time, it had been a while, and Tom was slightly bigger than I was used to. My jaw was already starting to ache a little. I steadied myself with a hand on Tom's thigh, whilst the other held his shaft, moving my grip in time with the bob of my head. My nose just brushed the hairs nestling at the base, as I took him deep and when he hit the back of my throat, I gagged slightly and pulled back quickly. I was almost relieved when I felt Tom's fingers tangle in my hair and encourage me to release him. "Sorry, I–"

"Shh, shh, you were wonderful, too good actually, which is why I need you to stop."

Tom helped me back onto the bed, my movements not quite as easy as they used to be. I hated that my muscles already ached and everything felt like so much effort. I still had another thirteen weeks of this and Tom and I were just getting started. He positioned me at the top of the bed, carefully tucking pillows around me, and bending the leg furthest from him at the knee and letting it drop so I was open to him. All of this was done, with little kisses, and whispers of affection. Then he settled next to me and kissed me soundly.

Tom held me in place whilst he brought me to orgasm with his fingers. It didn't take long, and had I not been so caught up in the moment I might have been suitably embarrassed by just how quickly it had happened, how loud and wanton I sounded, or how ridiculously wet I was – honestly – I would have to change the sheets before I'd be able to sleep in this bed.

We slowed, just for a moment, long enough for me to come down from my dizzying high. But my heart was still racing, chest still heaving when Tom posed his next question, "How would you be most comfortable, I don't want to hurt you."

I was too blissed out to really understand what he was asking, but something must have clicked because I found myself sitting up. My back ached from laying flat for too long, so I started crawling to my knees. Tom caught on quickly. He helped me turn around completely and bent me over. He was painstakingly careful with me, as he encouraged my head to the mattress, turning my face gently to one side and ensuring I was comfortable, then he shuffled my knees forward so my arse was up in the air. I was allowed one hand to balance myself. The other he took by the wrist and pinned to my back, causing me to hiss in slight discomfort. "Is this okay?"

"Yes," I told him, despite the ache in my shoulder from the restraint.

"Good."

With one hand still firmly holding my wrist in place, he used the other to position and guide himself into me from behind. I couldn't quite believe the lewd noise that escaped me, somewhere between a grunt and a howl. Tom wasn't much better, I could hear his breathing become hoarse from the effort to keep it steady.

His first few thrusts were slow and calculated, allowing me to get used to him. But I was restless, and I whined impatiently. It wasn't registering that he was taking care not to hurt me, now I was in what he considered a more fragile state. But the noise I made caused him to snap his hips suddenly enough for me to yelp.

"Fuck, yes! Tom!"

The sound of his name on my lips seemed to spur him on and his movements increased both in speed and ferocity. Each impact hit me deeply, drawing gasps and curses from my lips. I nearly lost my balance when my arm was released, but I quickly found it again, now able to use both hands to brace myself. "Ada, Ada, Ada..." Tom chanted my name, and that's when it started. My body trembled beneath him, and my vision went white. I could feel my walls contracting around him, squeezing him, as my channel convulsed through my second, blinding orgasm.

I might have screamed. I wasn't sure, I couldn't really remember. Nor could I clearly remember Tom finishing. But when I came too, I was no longer on my knees, but on my side. Tom's arms wrapped securely around me, holding me with my back pressed to his clammy chest.

"Are you alright?" the words came with a kiss to my shoulder.

"Yeah."

"I can be really intense I know, we probably should have discussed it before…"

"No."

"No?"

"I like it, Tom. How…intense you are."

"Hmm," Tom hummed and moved his legs to weave and tangle with mine. I looked down, catching sight of his socks, once again. The socks, which he'd been in such a hurry to get naked, he'd neglected to remove. They were black and covered with little multi-coloured stethoscopes. I giggled, "What?"

"Nice socks."

He wiggled his toes, "Secret Santa from a colleague last Christmas."

"Sexy."

"Why do you think I kept them on?"

CHAPTER FIFTEEN

Too good to be true

28 Weeks and 3 days

The day hadn't really got off to a good start. I woke up tired. Sleep was becoming more illusive as the discomfort of my ever-changing body and fidgeting baby was ruining my ability to get comfortable. My newly revived sex life probably also had something to do with my current state of perpetual fatigue.

I could hardly complain though. I was enjoying every single second of it.

Still, moments of deep set guilt would take over my entire consciousness daily. I shouldn't be so happy, not with this man. If it wasn't for him, I'd still have Dena. I couldn't hate him or blame him for any of it, not now. His affection was genuine, as was mine for him. I was starting to think it could really work, I could really see myself happy with Tom.

He'd cleared his spare room at the weekend and surprised me, when he took me inside and he'd started painting the walls a lovely duck egg blue. A boxed-up cot sat in one corner and the single bed protected in plastic covering was moved to the centre of the room. He told me that he wanted me to feel comfortable bringing to baby to stay at his place. That regardless of our relationship, I was welcome in his home even if we chose not to live together. It was a sweet gesture, and I was comforted by the idea of me and our little boy having somewhere we could call home. Even if not straight away, it showed me Tom's intentions and his commitment to not only fatherhood, but to me.

But I was still sad. Tom tried. I could see he did everything in his power to make me smile and it worked most of the time. But I knew it would be a long while before I'd be able to truly accept my life without Dena. I had other friends, not many. I tried to see other people, I always had, it wasn't like Dena was the only person I'd spent time with. But most of them were people I used to drink with, and attend gigs with, hardly any of them made reasonable company for coffee and had little interest in spending time with a pregnant woman.

The stress of the constant emotional turmoil was exhausting.

I was pleased with how things between Tom and I were progressing, but my contentment wasn't to last. There were still things which were a way off. I'd not met his family, although he had spoken to my Mum on the phone. Quite by accident, my Mum is saved under her name on my phone. So, when I was out of the room and he saw 'Joanne calling' on the screen he answered on my behalf to explain I couldn't get to the phone. By the time I'd finished in the shower, he'd been pulled into a twenty-minute long conversation with my Mum and had accepted a weekend invitation for us to stay with them in Brighton for a fortnights time. I was livid.

That spurred our first argument.

I wasn't ready to meet his family or have him meet mine. Even though in less than three months we'd have a baby together, we'd only been seeing each other for less than a month. I knew 'meet the parents' would have to happen before the baby arrived, but I was hoping we could hold off a little longer. The fact that he'd taken it upon himself to accept the invite to my parent's home angered me and I made sure he knew just how much.

"You've what?" I set down my mobile phone which he'd just handed back to me on his kitchen counter.

"I thought it sounded like a good idea, we're going to have to meet each other's families eventually. It was lovely of her to invite me to their home –"

"Yes of course it was lovely, because she's my Mum, of course she wants to meet you! For fucks sake! Are you stupid?"

"Ada –"

"No, don't! Don't use that voice, it's not going to work, Tom! I'm fed up of this, you dictate everything about this relationship, and it's not fair!"

"Now, hang on a minute –"

"No, I won't hang on a minute! Having me at your heel in the bedroom is one thing Tom, but I do have a voice in this relationship. This was not your decision to make, don't you get that? You should have consulted me and asked me if it was okay."

"Alright, okay, I'm sorry...we'll call her back..."

"No, you won't, because that's just you getting another one over on me. It makes me look like the bitch, so don't even go there!" I huffed and picked up my phone again, then stomped into the bedroom to collect my bag.

"What are you doing, Ada?"

"I'm going home, I think we're spending a bit too much time together."

"Don't be ridiculous, you can't leave."

"Oh, I'm ridiculous now, am I?"

"That's not what I meant."

"It's exactly what you meant!"

"I don't want you to leave, Ada."

"Have you even been listening to me? This is not about what you want, Tom!" I screamed at him, and I had to give it to him, he didn't shout back. He stayed calm and took it as I called him over-bearing and controlling and a host of other names which I didn't mean and would later regret. I was horrible, mean and spiteful.

Finishing my screaming fit, I'd made a hasty exit from his flat and caught a cab home. That was two days ago. We had spoken since. I'd apologised for my reaction and he'd apologised for not consulting me. He admitted that he was worried he'd lost me and I wouldn't want to see him anymore. I was overcome with guilt, because I was still very much smitten, and I assured him that we were fine.

I'd not seen him since though. He had a busy week at work, with a twelve-hour shift in A&E and then more patient hours than normal due to a colleague being on holiday. Then I was working, a day in the studio, then a full day of meetings in London. Then the rest of the week I'd be working at home. I'd told Tom it would do us good to have a few days apart. He'd been hesitant, insisting he would still be able to come over after work, but I adamantly refused. I hated that we'd argued so soon into our relationship and I could only read this as a bad sign. Space would do us good, even if he didn't agree with me.

In hindsight, I should have been more concerned by my increased fatigue. I'd mentioned it to the midwife at my check up the previous day. My blood pressure had been lower than normal, but she was not concerned. It was normally a tad on the high side, so the fact that it had dropped was positive. I mentioned the tightening pains I'd been getting over the past twenty-four hours. Regular, every few hours and lasting several minutes. Braxton Hicks – that's what she told me, they commonly started in the second trimester and I'd just hit my third. My baby boy was still measuring big, but he always had so again she was not worried. His heartbeat was nice and strong. Perfectly healthy, she said.

Being sent on my way with a full bill of health for me and my baby was probably why I brushed it off when I woke up several times in the night with stabbing pains in my lower back and those increasingly familiar tightening's in my tummy. But the baby was kicking away, and the discomfort soon died down, so I settled back to sleep.

The next day, on top of the tiredness I'd woken up with, sitting at my mixing desk was uncomfortable. I found myself taking frequent breaks to walk around my tiny flat. My back was constantly throbbing and the pains in my stomach were coming on so strong that they took my breath away and I found myself gripping onto nearby table tops and doorframes for support. But I still didn't worry. I was in my third trimester, it was meant to get harder. I told myself I should count my blessings that I'd had an easy, comfortable pregnancy so far.

Then I noticed the blood.

Lauren Hope

It wasn't much and it was only there when I wiped. It was enough to stain the toilet tissue and enough to frighten me into calling the Maternity Triage at the hospital. I was asked a few questions and the kind Midwife on the end of the phone told me to pack a small bag and slowly make my way to the hospital. She told me not to worry, or rush and to call back if the bleeding or pain worsened.

I tried to call Tom first, as I packed a change of clothes and a couple of toiletries. His mobile phone went to voicemail. So, I left him a simple message, telling him not to worry, but once he'd finished work to call me, and that I was going to hospital.

It was when I was dialling for a taxi that I felt the dampness between my legs, seconds before a cramp hit me, so severe it brought me to my knees. The pain passed quickly, and I scrambled to the toilet and found my knickers and leggings soaked through with bright red blood.

I did my best too stay calm, whilst I changed my clothes and put a pad in my knickers. Then I called the Triage line back. I told them the bleeding had worsened. The lady on the phone immediately told me to forget the taxi, and to stay put as she would be sending an ambulance. She offered to stay on the phone, but I told her I needed to contact my family and let them know where I was going. I assured her I would call back if I needed to. I was advised to leave my front door unlocked, and I gave her the building entry code for the paramedics.

Then I tried to call Tom again. As soon as I heard his voicemail I hung up and dialled his secretary's number. Sheila, who Tom complained about on an almost daily basis, told me Dr Cambridge was with patients and could not be disturbed. Tom hadn't told me what his situation was at work regarding my pregnancy and whether they knew about the baby and I didn't want to put my foot in it. I tried to tell her it was urgent, but the

188

best I got was her assurance that when he was next available she would let him know I'd called.

I didn't want to call my Mum and Dad. My Mum was not the best person to have in any kind of crisis. She had a habit of panicking and the thought of her jumping in the car and breaking speed limits down the M23 turned my stomach. The only person I really wanted now, was Dena.

I called Matt. But like Tom, his number when to voicemail, so I tried his secretary. I was in luck, he was available, and my call was passed through.

"Ada, you know it's not appropriate to call me at work –"

"I need to speak to Dena, I need you to call her!"

"Ada –"

"Matt, I'm bleeding, and I'm waiting for an ambulance and I need her. Please!" It was the first time I'd felt truly panicked and I knew my voice would be telling. I was alone, and I was scared.

"Fuck, Ada…I'll call her. Is it bad, are you in pain?" I could practically hear him springing into action. Matt knew me well enough to know I wouldn't be asking for his help unless this was serious.

"It's bad enough for them to send an ambulance and… fuck –" I hissed as another severe cramp doubled me over to my hands and knees. I dropped my mobile to the floor and it landed on it's face a little way, away from me. When I looked down, I was horrified to see blood soaking my maternity jeans and spreading rapidly through the denim.

"Ada?" Matt's voice was muffled and I reached for my phone.

"Matt…" My voice was trembling, "It won't stop, it hurt's and it won't stop."

"Alright, Darling," His voice was calm, but it didn't help my fear, "I'm calling Dena now. When I hang up I'd like you to call triage back and tell them what you've told me, okay?"

"Okay."

"Stay calm, and breath, yes, Darling?"

"Thank you."

"I love you, Ada."

"I love you too Matt…Matt?"

"Yes love?"

"I can't get a hold of Tom."

"Alright. I'll see what I can do."

Everything that happened next was a blur. A vague memory.

I was bleeding so heavily and in such severe pain that I couldn't move myself from the floor. I did manage to call the triage team back, and I was distantly aware of someone speaking to me, calmly, urging me to keep talking.

I sort of remembered the paramedics arriving.

I remembered Dena's voice, I think I was in the ambulance at the point. I knew she was there, she'd come. Her hand squeezed mine, and she kept her face close to me, murmuring words of comfort, assurance that she was there and she wasn't going to leave me.

Then everything went black.

CHAPTER SIXTEEN

All at once

I didn't come around with a start, like you often see in medical dramas or read about in books. My rousing was slow, and I think it probably happened over several hours. It was like waking from a long and restful sleep.

The first time I properly woke I was aware of a dull ache in my lower body. My hips felt like they were being weighed down and my legs felt like they were made of lead.

"Ada?" the voice was quiet, a hesitant whisper and it took a great deal of effort to turn my head and look to my right. Dena was sitting there, her big brown eyes, wider than normal, were red rimmed and filled with concern.

"Dee…" My voice was croaky.

"Shush, shush, your throat will be sore from the anaesthetic," she told me quickly and then she shuffled her chair closer to the bed and picked my hand up in hers. My hand which I quickly realised was fitted with a canula, and a long plastic tube pumping something red into me. Blood.

She pressed her lips to my knuckles, "I'll get the nurse…"

"Don't..." I croaked again, frustrated that I speaking was such hard work, "Don't leave me."

"I'll only be a second –"

"Please."

"I promise, I'm not leaving, it's just outside," She squeezed my fingers and carefully lay my hand back down on the bed, before hurrying out of the room.

My head was fuzzy. I couldn't quite process what was going on. I was in hospital. I gradually took in my surroundings. A small room, a window to my left, and it was light outside, but I could only see the sky from where I lay, and that was through the gaps in the vertical blind. A chair each side of my bed. A table was to one side of me, with a jug of water and a few cups. Nothing more.

Then it occurred to me. Horror filled me, and I thought I might choke, as my breathing became shallow, and with all the effort I could manage I moved my left hand to my stomach. My baby.

Dena re-entered the room, followed by a lady wearing scrubs and a friendly smile. "It's nice to finally have you back with us, Miss Bloom."

I didn't answer. Although I didn't think she expected me to. She bustled around me for several minutes, checking a monitor, my blood pressure, and then she lifted a clipboard from the end of my bed and scribbled some notes. All the while Dena held my hand, quietly letting the woman do her job.

"A doctor will be down shortly to explain everything to you. If you can manage it would be good to sit up a little more, and try and have a few sips of water, it will help your throat," the seem-ingly kind nurse told me.

I blinked, the only thing I could really manage through the blind panic going on inside my head. I noticed her glance down and look to wear my hand still rested over my tummy. Her eyes softened, and she looked to Dena and gave a little nod. "I'll leave you two alone, I'll let Ada's family know she's awake, so they can make their way down. Although it's best not to have too many people in here at once," She looked back to me, "You need your rest."

"Ada, look at me, babes," I turned my head again, she smiled a small and encouraging smile. I didn't want to ask. I didn't want to know, it was better if I just didn't know. But I acknowledged her, "There's a good girl," she reached out with her free hand and brushed my hair out of my face.

I couldn't speak and I could feel my eyes welling with tears. Then, as if my body acted of its own accord a shuddering sob found its way out of me. I winced as my shoulders jerked forward and I tried to lift my hands to wipe the tears which had started to uncontrollably stream down my cheeks.

"Woah, woah, Ada," Dena acted quickly, brushing my tears away and gently wrapping her arms around me, being careful as possible not to hurt me in the process, "Don't cry, please don't cry."

"I...I..." I gasped, trying to say...anything.

"He's beautiful, Ada," Dena held my face in her hands and kept her face in front off mine, as if she wanted to make sure I understood what she was saying. "He's so very, very tiny, but he's perfect."

"He...my... where is he?" I choked the words out, a combination of relief and panic surging through me all at once.

"Shh, shh," she attempted to calm me, "Your baby boy is in

the Neonatal Unit. He's...he's too small at the moment, Ada. He needs a lot of extra help; his lungs aren't very strong yet. The Doctors are taking very good care of him."

I searched her face for any sign she might me protecting me by holding something back. But she wasn't.

"The doctor says you had a Placental Abruption... sometimes they aren't bad and are treatable throughout pregnancy, but yours was bad. Really bad, you've lost a fuck tonne of blood, you're really poorly."

"How long?"

"Two days."

"You're here."

"Of course, I am...fuck I wish... I'm sorry, Ada. I mean, I was pissed, like really pissed, but I never wanted to lose you. I love you."

I sniffled, trying to control the tears which just seemed to show no signs of stopping, "I love you too."

"Your Mum's here, she's with Baby, we've sort of been taking shifts, because we didn't want to leave you on your own. Your Dad and Matt have just gone to pick Toby up from the airport, he'll be here soon, he got the first flight he could."

"Toby's coming?" it must be bad if my brother was flying from California.

"I thought I was going to lose you..."

"What?"

"You should have seen yourself... you turned grey! I thought you...I was so scared."

Then it struck me. There was one person she hadn't mentioned yet.

"Where's Tom?"

Her eyes narrowed, and she let go of me, sitting back in her chair, "He," she almost spat the word, "Is with your Son."

He was here, at the hospital, with our baby. That's where he was meant to be. What reason did Dena have to speak of him with such distain in her voice? But it didn't really matter right now, I really couldn't give a shit about whatever Dena's beef with Tom was. There was just one thing I cared about.

"When can I see my baby?"

The Doctor visited me and seemed to speak for ages. He told me in detail the severity of what had happened to me. The blood being pumped into me was my second transfusion. I had suffered from major haemorrhaging and lost over two thirds of my bodies blood supply. I would like need a further transfusion before my energy levels started restoring themselves.

I learnt that when the paramedics arrived I'd been drifting in and out on consciousness. I'd been able to speak, although I had no recollection of this. I lost full consciousness on the journey to the hospital. My baby was monitored and was in a lot of distress and the only way to attempt to save either of us was for an emergency c-section.

Unfortunately, he could not tell me as much about the current health of my baby, although he assured me that the doctors taking care of him in Neonatal would visit me when I was feeling stronger, to talk to me in detail. But I was assured that he was a little fighter. It didn't do much to settle my worries though, I knew doctors avoided definite answers when things could go either way.

What was most distressing though was the news that I would not be allowed to leave the ward at least until I'd had another two pints of blood pumped into me. The baby being brought to me was not an option either.

"I want to see him," I sobbed the words to my Mum after the Doctor left, "I need to see him."

"I know, Love."

"Please can you speak to them, I'll be okay, I'll go in the wheelchair, I could take the drip with me."

"Ada, you are still very poorly, and your little man needs you to be as strong as possible."

I sniffed, "Is Tom still with him?"

"Tom hasn't left his side," that was news to me, I knew he'd been there, but I hadn't realised that it was constant. "He's a lovely man, Ada."

"You...you've spoken to him?"

"Well, he's not really up to having a real chat at the moment. But yes, we've spoken a little. His Mother and I have been encouraging him to take a walk and eat. He...he's worried sick about you."

"He is?"

"Of course, but… well we all thought it best he stayed with the baby," I frowned.

"Yes, of course…but… does he know I'm awake?"

"Yes, I was with him when the Nurse called up."

"Did you say his Mum is here?"

"Yes, she came last night and has been with him today, I've not had chance to meet her properly," Mum explained. Very suddenly I felt quite overwhelmed and I knew another round of tears was just around the corner. Why was everyone meeting my baby before me? I knew Tom's Mum was family but…I didn't even know her. It wasn't fair. But I couldn't even be cross about it. My shoulders jerked as sobs wrecked through me, and my Mum took my hand and tried to comfort me. I didn't have to tell her what was wrong. She just knew.

It was another twenty-four hours before my Doctor gave the nursing staff the all clear to allow me to leave the ward for a short while in order to visit my baby. It was under the strict circumstances that I travelled there in wheelchair, and it would have to be long enough after my dose of pain medication that the drowsy effects had worn off, but not so late that I'd be uncomfortable and in need of my next dose. That gave me a very small window, but I was taking it.

One of the nurses had helped me take a shower. It had been a painful and embarrassing ordeal. Standing and sitting was agony due to the fresh stitches in my stomach. I was also bleeding, which I was finding more distressing than necessary. I knew bleeding after childbirth was normal, but it had not occurred to me that after a c-section at almost twenty-nine weeks this would still happen. I was two days post-partum and soaking through pads every couple of hours. The energy it took to get up and down to the bathroom, not to mention the humiliation of needing help with each and every trip, was wearing me down emotionally.

Dena had been sweet enough to go to my flat and collect some home comforts. This included a pair of baggy pyjama bottoms which wouldn't aggravate my stitches and my favourite baggy band t-shirt. She had forgotten to bring my shampoo and conditioner which meant I was using the stuff the hospital supplied and it had turned my hair into a dry frizzy mess. I somehow tamed it into a messy knot on the top of my head.

I looked a state. Honestly. I'd seen myself in a mirror and I was pale, more so than normal, and my eyes had ghastly bluish grey bags beneath them. My lips were chapped, and I could feel how sore they were. But I was seeing my baby, and I didn't care how I looked.

My Mum took me to the Neonatal Unit. She pushed me in a wheelchair borrowed from the ward. I didn't feel good, but I wasn't about to go telling anyone just how weak I felt. Nothing bad was going to happen to me, I just needed to get to my baby. As soon as I'd seen him, and I knew he was okay I'd be able to rest some more. It wasn't far, down the corridor and up one lift to the next floor. You had to ring a buzzer to be granted entry and slather yourself in hand sanitiser.

The first thing that struck me about Neonatal is that it was quiet and dark. The windows all had vertical blinds which were turned to allow in minimal sunlight. It was a little bit like walking into a library, you felt speaking in anything above a whisper would get you immediately shushed.

We turned a corner and I saw Tom before he saw me. He was sitting in a chair against the wall in the corridor and he was looking into his lap. There was a woman sitting next to him, she was small with white hair, and she appeared to be talking to him. She was leaning in close and I could see her lips moving. Tom's head moved in small nods to acknowledge her. The woman didn't seem to notice our approach and we were almost in front of them by the time Tom looked up.

His eyes met mine, and it was like he didn't recognise at first. His brow creased into ever such a slight frown, and a second later his already tired, red eyes flooded with tears, "Ada."

"Hi," I whispered. I wanted out of the wheelchair, I wanted to just fall into his arms and hold him. He looked exhausted, almost as bad as me. His skin was pale and his face puffy. His hair was a little bit greasy and very dishevelled, as was his beard.

"Oh god, Ada," he choked his words this time, and almost fell from his chair as he moved to kneel in front of me, taking my hands in his, careful not to knock my canula. "I'm so sorry, I've been so worried. I couldn't answer your call, and I wasn't there –"

"Please don't...Tom...stop," I pleaded as tears spilled from my own eyes. I'd cried more in the past twenty-four hours than I had in my entire adult life, and I was surprised there was anything left in me. "You were here, you came, it's okay, I'm okay... where...why are you out here?"

"Oh," He scrambled up, and acknowledged my Mum with a nod, then pulled my wheelchair by its arm so I was next to his chair, and he sat back down. He took hold of my hands again. "The doctors are with him."

"Why, is something wrong?" my chest tightened with panic.

"No, no, it's just routine checks, there's not a lot of room in there," he nodded at the door next to us, and I realised that was where he was. My baby was just on the other side of that wall. Tom squeezed my hands in his reassuringly, "He's perfect, Ada."

"I want to see him," I returned the grip Tom had on my hands.

"Not long, Darling. They'll be out in a moment…" he trailed off, and I think he remembered at the same time I did, that we were not alone. He sat back a little, and looked to his left, "Erm… Ada…this is my Mum, Susan…Mum, this is Ada."

I looked to the women on Tom's left. I could see Tom in some of her features, mostly around her forehead, and brow. But that's really where the similarities stopped. I could see she was visually assessing me. She didn't have the same softness to her eyes as Tom did. In fact, she looked quite…I'm not sure, disappointed maybe? Disapproving? She wasn't happy with what she was looking at when she looked at me.

"Hello, Mrs Cambridge…"

"It's Ms. Cambridge…I've been divorced almost twenty-five years."

"Mum…" Tom's tone was warning.

"I'm sorry," I wasn't sorry, but I also wasn't sure what else to say. Tom's family's approval of me was the least of my worries at the moment, but I was concerned that my own Mother might make a scene should she hear anyone speak ill of me.

Fortunately, before we could speak anymore the door next to us opened and a woman leant out, smiling at Tom, then looking at me, "Are you Adelaide?"

"Ada," I nodded.

"Would you like to come and meet your Son?"

The room was small like Tom had said. Filled with machines, and the sound of a steady beep from one of the monitors, I wasn't sure which one. A couple of chairs were pushed to the edge of the room, and in the middle was an incubator. A big plastic box, tubes and wires coming from all over it. It was slightly too high up for me to see in, when my wheelchair was pushed into the room by Tom. Mum and Susan waited outside, and the other nurses who had been inside left, so it was just us and the Doctor.

"Tom, can you help me up?" he looked down at me hesitantly, "I'm okay, I can't see him."

Slowly, and very carefully Tom helped me from the wheelchair, into a standing position. Once up, I could move easier. That's when I saw my baby for the first time.

He was tiny and very pink. But he looked like a real baby. He wore only a tiny nappy and a little white hat on his tiny head, which from his position on his back, rested slightly towards me. His knees were bent up and his arms were up by his head. He was covered in various cables. Monitoring wires stuck to his little chest, and tubes came from his nose and were secured in place by some tape. But beneath everything, he was just as Tom had said, absolutely perfect.

I gripped onto Tom's arm as I learnt closer to get a better look, my tears freefalling and splashing to the floor beneath me.

"We've just checked him all over, he's doing very well. But he still has a very long way to go," the Doctor started gently. "I know your Doctor has explained to you what happened, Ada... the birth was extremely traumatic, for you and for your baby boy. He was starved of oxygen for some time. At the moment his lungs aren't strong enough to work completely on their own, so we are just helping him along until they are."

"How long?" I asked, not taking my eyes off my baby.

"It's hard to say, he is getting stronger by the day, so we would hope not very long. He has a strong heart, as you can see from this monitor," I took my eyes off my baby boy long enough to look at the heart monitor, displaying a little even mountain range of green lines. I had no idea what any of it meant, but if the Doctor said it was good, and Tom wasn't worried then I could only take this to be positive. "Would you like to touch him?"

"Am I allowed?" I shot my eyes up to her hopefully, and then looked back at Tom, who nodded. The Doctor stepped in to open a little circular window at the side of the incubator. Hesitantly I reached in, until my finger could stroke the little hand. He moved when I did, his tiny fist unfurled, and his little fingers sought out my stroking finger and gripped onto it, barely wrapping around it. I was taken aback by the strength in his hold "Oh!"

"I'll leave you alone, but if you have any questions at all, or would like to talk about anything I'll be more than happy to come up to the ward and see you, Ada. I felt it was better you come here and see him first," I nodded, not looking up as the Doctor left, too enrapt by the tiny little miracle in front of me.

We were finally alone. Me, Tom and our little baby boy.

"I'm so glad you're here, Ada," I could feel Tom's breath on my neck, and his body warm next to mine. "I was so scared…"

"So was I."

"How do you feel? Really?"

"Awful, like I've been hit by a train. I feel sick and dizzy all the time. My stomach is so sore, and tight…" I finally withdrew my hand from the incubator and Tom closed the little door until it clicked shut. Only then did I turn into his arms, allowing him for the first time to hold me properly.

"Oh god, Ada," his face buried into my hair, and he held me tightly to his chest, "I thought I'd lost you."

"I'm not that easy to get rid of," I mumbled into his shirt, and through his tears, he managed a choked laugh.

CHAPTER SEVENTEEN

When all hope seems lost

I thought once I'd been able to see my baby I'd be able to relax more. But I was wrong. Once I'd seen him I didn't want to leave. But I'd had to. Tom had held me in that tiny room for just over an hour before I could no longer hide the pain I was in. I needed morphine and I needed sleep.

I'd cried when Tom had eased me back into the wheelchair. From the pain and from desperation of not wanting to leave my baby. Tom didn't know what to do, that was clear, he looked so torn.

"I wish I could come back up with you but..."

"You need to be here."

"You need to rest, you aren't well enough to be leaving your bed. Please try not to worry about him, the Doctors are doing an amazing job and I promise I won't leave him," Tom assured me, squeezing my hand.

"What about you?"

"What about me?"

"You need to rest, you look so tired and you need to shower."

"I'm alright, Ada. You worry about getting better, okay?" I nodded, a small weak nod as he wheeled me back to the door and opened it. My Mum stood from her seat next to Tom's Mum. It looked like they'd be discussing something and the look on my Mum's face told me whatever it was, she was not happy about it. But she quickly plastered on a smile when she saw me.

"He's beautiful, isn't he?" She asked, another small nod.

"Make sure she goes straight back to bed, and she needs more pain killers," Tom instructed my Mum, but his tone was gentle, and concerned.

"Of course, Doctor Cambridge," Tom forced a smile at my Mum's attempt to lighten the mood. Then he looked to me again. A reassuring smile, then he disappeared back into the room, the door closing softly behind him. His Mum stood up quickly and moved to follow her Son into the room, without speaking to, or even looking at me.

"Ms. Cambridge..." she stopped and looked down at me. She had to because I was in a wheelchair, but the look in her eye suggested, she genuinely thought me beneath her. "I'm sorry we haven't been able to meet properly yet, I know the circumstances are..." *No, I wasn't getting into this now. I couldn't.* "Thank you for being here for Tom and our baby."

"He's my son," she answered simply, before disappearing into my own son's hospital room.

"I don't like that woman," my Mum muttered as we left the ward, but I didn't react. I was too tired and in too much pain to really care what she thought of me, or what my Mum thought of her.

"Ow, ow, ow!" I whined as Dena helped me into a fresh pair of pyjama's the next day. She'd insisted on being the one to help me in the shower and freshen up, after I'd been so upset by the nurse having to help me the previous day.

"I'm sorry, I'm trying to be careful."

"I know, I'm just so sore."

"Do you need more Morphine? I'll get the nurse."

"I don't know," I sighed miserably. I'd already been told that morning by the Doctor that I wouldn't be allowed off the ward today. I'd had a bad night, my blood pressure had dropped dramatically, and I'd been sick. I'd overdone it, and I was still feeling the effects today.

"Toby was visiting the baby this morning," I could tell Dena was trying to brighten the mood. The previous morning my brother had come to see me, having slept off his jet lag and my Mum and Dad not being able to keep him away from me a minute longer. He didn't go to see the baby though. He told me he couldn't possibly see my baby before me and his primary concern was to see that I was alright. As soon as he knew that, then he could wait. I loved him for that.

"I know," I mumbled.

"You know, he doesn't have a name yet..." Dena trailed off, she was broaching that subject carefully.

"No."

"No, he doesn't have a name? Or no you don't want to talk about it?"

"Tom and I hadn't decided, we were doing lists."

"Ah," she responded shortly, and turned away from me in a deliberate action, whilst pretending to tidy up around herself.

I huffed and shifted myself attempting to get comfortable. It didn't work, and I let out a long-pained groan, just as the nurse entered the room.

"It sounds like someone's in a lot of pain," the little blonde lady commented, as she approached and picked up my chart, "We keep telling you, Ada. There's no shame in accepting help in the form of medicine. Your body has been through a lot of trauma and you're already doing far too much."

"It's not that kind of pain, it's –" I stopped, hesitant as to how serious this was and if I really wanted to admit it, "It's my chest, I feels uncomfortable. Really heavy and hot."

"Your chest, or…your breasts?" the nurse came a little closer to the top end of my bed.

At her words, I brought my right hand to my chest and moved it carefully over my pyjama covered breasts, wincing at the slight pressure, "My boobs."

"Well, I'll get a midwife to come and see you, but I'd say that's a good sign that your milk is coming in," she explained, with an optimistic smile.

"Really?" suddenly my aching body didn't make me feel quite so low. If my body was making milk, then it was doing something right. Which meant I wasn't completely failing my baby.

"Yes, it can take a little longer to come in after a c-section, if at all, especially given such an early birth. But seeing your little man yesterday has probably triggered a hormonal boost. You know...I will get a midwife to come and speak to you, but if we can get you to express a little bit of Colostrum, and start syringe feeding your baby, it might...it's not like a miracle cure, but... it wouldn't do any harm. The Neonatal doctors always prefer a baby to be on breastmilk and only topped up on formula if possible. It's gentler on delicate tummies," I listened intently as she explained this to me.

I hadn't wanted to breastfeed. It was actually the first thing I put in my birth plan. The whole thing had never appealed to me. I couldn't think of anything worse. I had big boobs as it was, and there was no way I could discretely feed a baby in public. I knew other women who'd successfully exclusively breastfed their infants for a decent amount of time, and I admired them for it. But, although it might work for them, the idea of it had always made my skin crawl, no it wasn't for me.

But...my body was making milk. My baby was poorly, and there was nothing I could do for him. Except this.

The midwife came and she taught me first how to express by hand. I couldn't believe it when that first bead of almost translucent fluid leaked from my nipple. It wasn't comfortable, but it wasn't difficult, and once it started it was easy to collect in a little syringe.

At the news that I was open to the idea of introducing my breastmilk to my baby's diet, my Mum had gone out and purchased one of those electric pumps. A big scary looking thing, which reminded me of what they attached to cows to milk them. When set up it made an unsettling humming noise and I was hesitant to attach it to myself. However, the midwife was eager to get me using it, as it would encourage breast milk production.

My milk was taken away and I was assured when I was well enough to see my baby again I'd have the opportunity to try feeding him by syringe. Then, when he was strong enough, if I wished to I could attempt latching him to the breast.

"How are you feeling?" my Mum asked the question, just as I'd gotten comfortable again, having expressed for the third time that day.

"Actually, a little bit better," I admitted, "The midwife said that sometimes when milk comes in it can make you feel a bit..flu-ish."

"Well that's good, you look better. A bit more colour to your cheeks."

There was a light tap on the door and we both turned. I wasn't expecting anyone. Dad and Toby had popped by for a short while after spending the morning with the baby. Then left just after lunch. I'd made Dena promise to go home and rest and spend some time with Matt, as she had hardly left the hospital.

The door eased open and my nurse popped her head round the door, "You have a visitor, can he come in?"

"Erm..." I wasn't sure who to expect, so when the door opened fully, and Tom was standing behind the nurse, looking a bit fresher than the previous day, and very sheepish, I couldn't help but grin at him.

"I suppose so," I teased. He beamed at me as he came into the room, and didn't hesitate to stride over to me, lean down and press his lips to my forehead, cupping my face in one of his large hands as he did. He'd been careful the previous day, he had not kissed me, just held me and comforted me in the only way he could. But now his affection for me was clear. "What are you doing here?"

"Mum and Natalie are with him, they told me to go and get something to eat but...well I snuck up here, I had to see you again."

"Tom..." my Mum's voice pulled us apart.

"Matt told me him and Dena were going home for a bit," Tom explained, ad if already knowing what she was about to say.

"Yes, but... well I don't want any trouble," Mum was still wary.

"I promise, Jo, if there's any trouble, it won't be me causing it. I just need to spend a little bit of time with my girlfriend," he glanced between us, then landed his eyes back on me and gave my hand a reassuring squeeze.

"I'm still your girlfriend?" I had to cut in, because to be quite honest, in amongst all my other worries, the argument Tom and I had, had the last time we'd seen each other was still hanging over my head.

"Well...I hope so," Tom frowned.

"Yes, I am," I gave him a relieved smile.

"Look, I'm going to grab some food in the café, and give you two a bit of time together. Would you like anything, Tom?" Mum stood and pushed her chair back as she did.

"Can you grab me a sandwich or something. I'm not fussy on fillings," Tom straightened himself up.

My Mum left us alone, and the second the door shut, Tom was dragging the chair right up to the bed, so he could sit next to me.

"How is he? The doctor said he wants me to rest a couple of days before I leave the ward again, I was really sick last night."

"I heard, darling. I'm so sorry, how do you feel now?"

"Better, it was my milk coming in, and the fact that I'm still low on energy from the blood loss making me feel rubbish...did you get to feed him?"

"No, they're tube feeding for now. But...well he's doing amazing. The doctor visited again this morning and she said they are going to try taking him off the oxygen for short periods tomorrow, which means...well if your doctor will let you visit, you'll be able to hold him."

"I don't care I he lets me, Tom. I'll discharge myself!"

"Ada, you'll do no such thing. I won't hold him before you. I promise, I want you to hold him first. You know the nurses offered to let me change a nappy and I didn't even want to do that before you! Also, he's so tiny, I'm a little scared of hurting him."

"He's your son Tom. If I can't come tomorrow and you're allowed to hold him, you should," I said the words, but I wasn't sure I meant them. I did want to be the first person to hold my baby. Even though doctors and nurses had got there before me. But at the same time, Tom had been the one sitting vigil by his incubator for four days. "I just...I feel so helpless, I want to be there. I've only seen him once and I miss him. I miss feeling him in my belly. When he was in there and I could feel him kicking around I knew he was alright. Until he wasn't... I just feel like... I'm failing him."

I took a shaky breath and willed myself not to cry.

"Ada! You're not failing him. You're doing all you can, your body has been through a serious and traumatic ordeal. You have a lot of recovering to do, they may have pumped blood back into you, but you've still had emergency surgery. Your body is healing from pregnancy and you're adjusting to becoming a mother, without being able to bond with your child. On top of all that, you're sitting up here expressing breastmilk and I know you didn't want to breastfeed, so you're doing it because you feel it's the only thing you can do for him right now. That's amazing, Ada. All I can do is sit there helplessly," Tom shifted, quite swiftly, from his chair to the edge of my bed. "And when you came out of surgery, they said it was touch and go, that you'd lost so much blood, and I couldn't see you. Then they took me into this room and there was this tiny little helpless baby, and fuck...I was terrified. I still am. I had no idea what to do, and I felt like I'd failed both of you. If I'd been able to take your call, or if I hadn't been such an idiot I might have been with you the night before and known something was up."

"I don't blame you, Tom, I don't think you being there would have stopped this happening."

"I know," He took both my hands in his, "I was so terrified that you'd wake up and think I didn't care."

"What's going on? I'm not stupid. Has something happened between you and Dena?"

"Well, she's still cross with me..."

"But she's forgiven me! That's hardly fair. She does know about us, doesn't she? I mean I haven't said as much to her, but she must know we're...together?"

"Well, yes... I spoke to Matt. Who is still not very happy with me, but we're talking. I mean...he can see how much I care about you, and how much I love our little boy. He knows what I've been going through on that ward. But...Claudine doesn't think... well...it doesn't matter, she's not happy with me, and to be honest it's easier not to fight her. I don't want to fight anyone, I just want you and our baby to be okay. So, for now I've just let her have her way," Tom sighed, and shook his head.

"Her way?"

"It doesn't matter, Ada."

"It does matter! You haven't been up here because she wouldn't let you. That's what this is, everyone's been telling me you've stayed with our little boy, because you know that's what I'd want. But you know he's being well looked after, and as much as you don't want to leave him...you were worried sick about me."

"It's over now, Ada. Please don't worry about it."

"It wasn't her decision to make!"

"She is just looking out for you, Ada. You shouldn't be cross with her," Tom reached out to take both my hands.

"Stop being so damn nice all the time, Tom! It's lovely that she's here, but it took me almost dying and losing the baby for her to consider forgiving me. It's lovely that my Mum and Dad, and Toby, have all been here for me. But you're my boyfriend and the father of my child and to be honest the only person I've wanted here. No one had any right to stop you seeing me! I can't believe my Mum allowed it," I was cross, fuming.

"Ada, stop, darling. This is why no one told you. We didn't want you to get upset. It's not that she strictly forbid me from coming up here. Let me explain," Tom paused, and I calmed my breathing. I nodded permission for him to tell me what had happened,

"Claudine...well there was a bit of a scene in the family room. When I got here, she and Matt where there. You were still in theatre. The minute she saw me, she laid into me. She was so upset, and scared and traumatised by what she'd seen. I let her, because I was too shaken up to fight back. I don't even know half of what she said. Then, the Doctor came and told us you were out of surgery, but you were in ICU and the baby was being transferred to Neonatal. When Matt told them I was the Father, they lead me straight there, I wasn't given an option to see you. For the first twenty-four hours I was terrified of leaving the room. Then...your Mum and Dad came down. I asked if I could see you, if they were going to stay with him...they told me that for now it was best I didn't. That Claudine was very emotional and at everyone's throats."

I harrumphed, not completely satisfied, but feeling a little less angry.

"You should get back to him soon," I said the words quietly, my gut clenching at the thought of my little boy on his own, but conflicted because I didn't want Tom to leave me just yet. We'd just become parents and we'd hardly seen each other. We were both worried for our little boy, and we should be comforting each other.

"I've got a little while," it was like he was reading my thoughts.

"Would you lay with me?" I carefully shifted myself to the far edge of the bed, being careful not to hurt myself. I winced as my stitches pulled a little, but I managed to make a space next to me, "I just really need you to hold me, Tom."

No words were needed. Tom kicked his shoes off and carefully positioned himself next to me. He lifted his legs onto the bed and shifted around until he was able to wrap an arm carefully round my midsection, avoiding both my sore tummy, and sensitive boobs. I was more comfortable on my back, but I turned my head, so I could rest it on his shoulder. It felt good, comforting and safe. His smell, and his warmth surrounded me.

"I'm so happy you're here with me."

"Me too."

CHAPTER EIGHTEEN

Me against the world

"I saw Tom today," I told Dena as soon as she came into my room. She stopped dead next to my bed, putting the bag she had been carrying down on my table.

"I thought you weren't allowed off the ward?"

"I'm not, he came up to see me, whilst his Mum and Sister were with the baby."

"Oh," that was it. That was all she said, but I could tell there was a fire burning behind her eyes. She avoided my gaze as she started unpacking a little picnic of treats onto the table, "I brought my laptop and some goodies. I thought maybe we could watch a film."

"He's not going away, Dena. I know you're still pissed off, probably with both of us, but you can't put it all on him. He's my baby's Dad and he isn't going anywhere," I wasn't going to let her avoid this.

"You don't know that. He cheated on Grace. He only decided to be involved when I was out of the picture. He's not the most reliable person," there we go, the real reason. She was scared I was going to get hurt. I got that, from the outside Tom did not have the best track record.

"I know that's how it looks. But… you know he's actually been amazing. He cares about me so much. I care about him. We… I know he's not my usual type, but there was chemistry from the second we met. I really like him, he treats me well and…well it would be easier if you could not hold a grudge. Or just be civil at the very least…he is Matt's friend. You know he's a good man," my eyes followed her as she pottered around the room, opening the drawer next to me and putting some fresh pyjamas inside, and underwear. She'd obviously been to my flat again. I was pleased to see my bottles of shampoo and conditioner being placed on a shelf in the cupboard.

"I thought he was a good man…until he cheated on his pregnant girlfriend and knocked up my best friend. Then told her he'd have nothing to do with the baby," Dena scoffed.

"Well, I'm sure Tom will do his best from here on out to prove his sincerity. But he's my boyfriend and whether you like it or not, he's going to be around. I'd prefer it if you didn't make it difficult," I kept my voice level and I did my best not to upset her to a point she might leave me again, "I love you Dena. I'm so happy you're here, I'll always want you as part of my life. But… Tom's going to be part of it too."

"Fine," the word was stiff as it left her lips, "I'll try and be civil. I'm not promising to be best friends but… it's obvious he cares about the baby. Matt said he's been worried sick, he was crying. He's asked after you every time Matt's spoken to him."

"Thank you, Dena."

"What do you fancy watching then?"

Walking. I was actually walking. Not relying on a wheelchair, as I made my way down up to the Neonatal unit. My doctor was so pleased with how I was doing, he approved for me to take another visit to see my baby.

My brother was with me this time and I clutched his elbow as we took a slow walk along the corridor and went up in the lift.

"Have you thought of a name yet?" several people had asked me now. Firstly Dena, then my Mum and Dad. The nurses on the ward were keen to know what little Baby Boy Bloom, which he was currently known as, would be called.

"Not yet," I told my brother. "Tom and I haven't had time to talk about it."

"Maybe when you've held him, something will come to you?"

"Maybe," I mumbled, I was nervous. Tom had said I may be able to hold my baby, but I didn't want to get my hopes up. But also, I was scared about him being off the oxygen. What if he wasn't strong enough?

"Tom's a decent guy."

"You've met?"

"Yesterday morning, when me and Dad went to see the Baby. Not your usual type, but he seems like a good fella."

"Not my usual type? I've had one serious boyfriend."

"Who Tom is nothing like, if anything he is the complete opposite of Magnus."

"Did you see his Mum?"

"No."

"She hates me."

"Now I'm sure that's not true. You're impossible to hate, Ada. You are literally the nicest person in the world."

I laughed, "Yeah well, tell that to Ms. Susan Cambridge. I've corrupted her baby boy with unprotected sex, and –" I stopped dead, as we approached the ward. I could hear Tom's voice, and it was coming from a room to our right, the little sign above the door read 'Family Lounge'. I was about to tug Toby in that direction, when I heard a second voice. One I wasn't as familiar with, but I did recognise. But the words of that person were what caught my attention. I rested a hand over Toby's and looked up at him, indicating that I wanted to hear what was being said.

"She's nothing to you, Thomas. You made a mistake, and yes something amazing has come from it. Despite the circumstance, of course I love my Grandson. But…his Mother leaves a lot to be desired."

"You have hardly spoken two words to her! How can you cast judgement on her?"

"I don't need to speak to her, her appearance tells me loud and clear, all I need to know. She's a tattooed harlot, and I don't know what on earth you were thinking when you jumped into bed with that."

"Mum!" Tom sounded suitably affronted by his Mother's assumption of me, and of her son's behaviour "When have you ever been someone to judge based on appearance alone?"

"Since my son decides he's in love with a trampy, green haired... goth, is that what they call them? I'd have expected this when you were in University, but you are nearly forty years old. You need to grow up!"

"I'm thirty-seven, and I will not tolerate you talking about my girlfriend that way. You're right, I am in love with her. She's incredible. She has tattoos? So what? I love them. I think she's beautiful. I'd think she was beautiful regardless of her hair colour. Her appearance has no standing on her personality, or intellect, did you know she's a self employed Sound Engineer? Built her own business up from scratch, she can also sing, and play multiple instruments. she's insanely talented. She's sweet and kind, and so, so strong –" I was sure I heard Ms. Cambridge scoff. "What are you asking me to do, Mum? Chose between my family, and the mother of my child?"

"It's not a choice Tom. I'm telling you to end this infatuation, and focus on being the responsible parent, because that woman is ill-equipped..." I didn't hear the rest because Toby was in my ear.

"I'm going in, how fucking dare she, does she know who you are? Who Dad is? He could make sure she never gets to see her grandson ever again, he won't hesitate, Ada, you know he won't," I had to hold on to Toby's wrist tightly to stop him storming in.

"Don't. I can deal with this," I let go of his arm and slowly made my way to the door.

"Ada," Toby's voice warned. But I ignored him.

"Tom," I walked into the room, he was standing, and his back was to me. I saw his shoulder jerk, at the unexpected sound of my voice. He turned and attempted to smile. I approached and took his arm, I was shaking slightly, but it was from anger, not from weakness. But I kept calm, purposely tip-toeing up so I could brush my lips over his. He hummed quietly against my mouth.

When I was firmly back on my feet, I looked at Susan, "Ms. Cambridge… I think we might have got off on the wrong foot… I'm not really sure what I've done to offend you. I know the circumstances which brought Tom and I together were not… ideal. But I can assure you I'm very fond of your son. I adore him, actually," Tom's hand slid over mine and squeezed it gently. I was amazed she was still listening. But she didn't look pleased, her eyes had focused on our joined hands, and there was a little huff of disapproval. I powered on, regardless, "I know you don't approve, but I really hope we could get to know each other. I want you to know I'm not some evil witch trying to corrupt your son, he's very able to make his own decisions, in fact he does…regularly. I know I'm a bit…off beat, but I'm happy with the way I look, I don't really care what you think of my appearance. But I do care that you think the way I look affects my ability to provide a stable, loving home for my Son, and to dote on yours."

"I think…" Her eyes trailed up from our joined hands to my face, "That my son is blinded by infatuation. He always did have a flair for the dramatic. That's my fault I suppose," she turned her eyes up to Tom, "But…your baby is the only little person who matters right now. You're both adults, I do not, and will not ever approve of this…sham. But I'll keep my mouth shut for my Grandson."

"Ada, I'm so sorry…" Tom started, as we were finally told by the nurse that the Doctors had completed their daily checks and we could see our son. I'd urged Toby to leave the ward, and insisted I'd be okay with Tom. Simply because I didn't want him alone with Susan once Tom and I weren't there. But it had been a very tense and awkward few minutes as we'd all sat waiting together in the family lounge.

"It's not your fault," I told him firmly. I would not have him apologising on his Mum's behalf.

"She's never been like this before, she's normally so…accepting. She's very open-minded."

"Oh yeah, I can tell," I responded sarcastically.

"It doesn't change the way I feel about you."

"I don't want to talk about this now, Tom."

"So, Baby Boy Bloom is off the ventilator, he's still being closely monitored," the midwife explained to us, as she shut the door behind her. "He needs to stay in the incubator for warmth, but he can come out for short periods, as long as he is well swaddled, have you heard of kangaroo parenting?"

"Yes," Tom answered, before I could. The name gave me a good idea as to what it meant. "Swaddling against the mother's skin, the body warmth acts like a natural incubator."

"That's right," the midwife nodded, with a little smile. She started to open up the incubator, "He's just about ready for a feed too, I've got some of your milk drawn up in a syringe, Ada. Would you like to hold him first?"

I nodded silently, and she gestured to a comfortable reclining chair which had not been in the room the last time I'd visited. Tom helped me ease down into it, the pain was lessening each day, but I still ached, and the stiches still pulled. Tom pulled the chair up next to me. "Okay Mummy, if you could pop open the top few buttons of your pyjama top, we can pop him inside, so he can snuggle up to you. If you're wearing a nursing bra you might want to take it off. The blinds are drawn."

It was a bit of shifting about, and Tom had to help me unfasten my bra, and remove it from under my pyjama top. I attempted to shun any embarrassment, Tom had seen me naked many times now, but he'd not seen my new milk filled breasts, or the unflattering nursing bras, and breast pads. But he didn't react as he folded the bra on the side and made sure the pads stayed in place as they were not damp enough to replace just yet. He unbuttoned my top, and then fetched a blanket off the side, that had been put there ready.

"Now I've disconnected all the tubes, but they won't be removed for a little while, so you'll need to be careful of them, are you ready, Ada?" I nodded again. Then she was lifting my little boy from his bed, and as she did he made some little squawking sounds, unhappy to be disturbed, and probably hungry. She positioned him carefully, allowing me to cup my hands around him and slid him into place on my chest, whilst she supported his head until it could rest against me in my reclined position. I couldn't take my eyes off him. As soon as his warm, pink skin was against mine, he automatically curled into me. His little fists balled up and pressed into me, and he nuzzled the top of my breast, smelling my milk and looking for his food. I looked up briefly at Tom when he wrapped the blanket around us both, tucking it carefully around our son, so just his head peaked out.

"Can I?" Tom's hand hovered over the little bundle on my chest, and I nodded. Tom's hand rested over our son, his palm nearly the size of the little infant. Then he leant over and brushed his lips against my cheek, and murmured in my ear, "Congratulations, Mummy."

"Would you like some photos?" The midwife asked, and Tom answered for me, taking his phone from his pocket and handing it to her. But I didn't react as she snapped a few shots of us, far to busy being unable to draw my eyes from my baby boy.

The midwife helped me feed him a few drops of milk from the syringe. It was the first time he'd fed this way, as he'd been receiving all sustenance by tube. His little mouth had slurped, and he'd squeaked enthusiastically at his first taste of milk. He constantly pressed his head to my breast and the midwife told me that was a positive sign that he would be ready to latch sooner than expected. They would start using a dummy, so he could learn the sucking motion required, as he was too young to do this naturally right now.

Then Tom held him. Similarly, to me, the nurse suggested he removed his shirt, as body heat was the best way to keep the baby warm enough. Tom rested back in his chair with our tiny boy swaddled against his chest, sleeping soundly after he'd had his fill of milk.

The midwife left us for a little while, so we could spend some time alone...as a family.

"He needs a name," I whispered, as I always felt I needed to when I was somewhere so quiet. But also, being careful not to wake up my sleeping son.

"I know, we didn't have chance to do our lists," the baby stirred from the rumble of his Daddy's voice in his chest.

"You've spent more time with him, did you think of any names? I honestly don't know, but he's five days old now. Have you called him anything in your head, other than Baby Boy Bloom?" I smirked.

"I'm not... well...I don't know."

"There was something?"

"Kind of," Tom glanced and me and then peered down at the little bundle, "He looks so cosy, doesn't he? All snuggled up like this."

"He does, he's like a little teddy bear with that blanket all tucked up around him, just missing the furry ears," I reached out stroking a finger over the fine hairs on his head, too minimal to distinguish a colour yet, but it felt soft like velvet. Then I looked back at Tom, "Go on?"

"Well, it's funny you should say that…in my head… what do you think of Teddy?"

"Teddy…" I tested the name, as I continued to stroke my son's head. It felt natural, it suited him. I could hear myself cooing it as I rocked him to sleep at night.

"If you don't like it…"

"I like it," I agreed. "Teddy," I said it again.

"Teddy Bloom," Tom smiled, pleased that I approved of his name choice, "Hello, Teddy."

"No."

"Hmm?"

"Teddy Cambridge."

CHAPTER NINETEEN

No such thing as plain sailing

I was given the all clear for discharge after twelve days. It should have been sooner, but I suffered an infection in my surgery scar, and ended up on intravenous antibiotics for two days.

But finally, I could go home. Theoretically.

Teddy was going from strength to strength. Exceeding the doctors' expectations every step of the way, he was completely without oxygen after one week. After ten days he was moved from high dependency. Tom and I were told to take each day as it came, that it was a marathon, not a sprint. Firstly, Teddy was still being tube fed the majority of the time. He took some milk by syringe but could not take enough this way. The first step was to get him feeding on his own, from bottle or breast. Which meant despite being well enough to go home, I was hesitant to leave my babies side, just in case.

On top of my hesitancy to leave the hospital, I hadn't really discussed with my family where I intended to go. But they made it very clear that they had some ideas of their own.

"Matt's going to drive up here after work to collect your things and take them back to ours," Dena told me, matter of factly, as she sat next to me on the Neonatal Ward. Teddy now shared a large room with three other babies. It was a busy ward, with Mums, Dads and Grandparents flitting in and out all hours of the day and night. There were no strict rules on visiting hours for the parents of the babies in Neonatal.

"What, why?" I had been staring at Teddy, smiling to myself, as he fidgeted in his sleep.

"So your things are there. You can hardly go back to yours, for starters the commute to the hospital will be a nightmare, our place is much closer. I also can't imagine you'd want to be on your own for a while, you still have to take it easy –" I cut her off.

"When was this decided?"

"Well, I spoke to your Mum and Dad, they agree that my place is the best option until Teddy is strong enough to go home with you, then of course you'll move in with them –"

"Excuse me?" I interjected again, "My parents decided this? Did they?"

"Well we spoke about it a bit yeah."

"Thank you for running it past me," I huffed. Having been so unwell and relying on others so much help with basic things changes the way those closest to you treat you. My Mother had sheltered me constantly, not telling me what was going on between Tom's family and mine whilst I was on the ward. Dena treated me like I was too young to make informed decisions, she'd even gone as far as selecting from the hospital menu on my behalf when they took dinner and lunch orders. I'd not had the energy to argue with anyone. I'd just let everyone get on with it, whilst I focused on getting strong for my baby. But now, I was nearly there, and I was pissed off.

"It just makes more sense."

At that moment Tom appeared. For the first time he'd gone somewhere other than home and the hospital. He'd spent the morning with his boss. He had a lot of work to sort out, and he'd not been prepared to spend any time away from the hospital until I was well enough to be with Teddy on my own.

"Did you know about this?" I'm not sure why I felt the need to take it out on him. I knew it was unlikely he had any idea about anything. Dena wasn't actively starting conversation with him, and although my family liked Tom, they had very little time for his family. Therefore, any discussion involving what happens next would have been kept strictly between my parents and Dena.

"I...I don't know," Tom stopped dead, "I've literally just come straight from work, I haven't even stopped, am I supposed to know something?"

"Well, apparently I'll be moving in with Dena and Matt tonight," I informed him.

"You will?" the look on Tom's face was one of confusion, but I could also see a flash of disappointment, "Doctor Malik discharged you then?"

"Yep," I popped the 'P'.

"Jo and I just think whilst Teddy is still here it makes more sense for Ada to stay with me and Matt. She's got her room, her stuff, and it's like ten minutes from here, Matt could even drop you off on his way to work," Dena explained all this, only glancing at Tom to address him once.

"Well yes, I can see how that would be the sensible option," Tom pulled up a chair and sat down.

"Then, when Teddy is ready to go home, I'll be moving back to Brighton with my parents," I added. That's when Tom's expression changed, his eyes darkened, and his brow creased into a frown. He nodded slowly.

"I see," His voice was quiet, "Well, if that's what you need, Ada."

He was missing the point. Completely.

"No, it's bloody not what I need," I snapped, "Thank you for your hospitality Dena, but I'll be going home with Tom tonight and when Teddy is well enough to come home, he will also be living at Tom's."

I hoped I'd made my point very clear, but I could see the hurt in Dena's face. What the hell was I meant to do? I loved her dearly, but she needed to understand that Tom was my boyfriend, and Teddy was our child. I wasn't going to be anywhere Tom wasn't.

"I'm going for some air," Dena stood up sharply. I knew when she was on the verge of losing her temper, and she'd already been told off once for raising her voice on the ward. I didn't chase her, she needed to cool down and see things clearly.

"Ada, you know if you want to stay with Dena and Matt, that's alright," Tom moved from his chair to the one next to me which Dena had vacated, "But I don't think I could bare you moving away with Teddy."

"I've got no intention of moving away. I don't want to stay with Dena and Matt either... I want to be with you. I need to be with you," I tried to assure him, "I'm sick of everyone thinking they can make decisions for me."

"I'm sure they're just looking out for your best interests."

"How is it in my best interests to tear my family apart, because that's what you are now, you and Teddy. You're both mine, and no one seems to get it. It's like they aren't taking us seriously. We're both adults, we have a baby together. We're getting through all this, together."

"Ada, love, remember how new to them this is? We know what we are, but to everyone else your family, my family, Dena and Matt, everyone... we've only been seeing each other a few days. It's easy for them to either forget you aren't on your own anymore or think I might not be willing to take on that responsibility."

"Come off it, Tom. Dena just wants to spite you right now...and well... my Mum likes you well enough, but that hardly matters because she thinks your Mum will be a poisonous influence in Teddy's life. She'd sacrifice my happiness in a heartbeat, if it meant your Mum was eradicated from our lives...I'm sorry," I knew what I'd said sounded harsh.

"Don't be sorry, my Mum has been awful to you. I'm barely on speaking terms with her myself...but she's coming around. Slowly."

"I don't want to be the reason you and your Mum fall out."

"You aren't, she is. Trust me, I think she just needs to get used to the idea that this isn't a faze, in much the same way your family do. Once she realises you aren't going anywhere, I know her opinion of you will change, she will want to get to know you."

I just nodded and leant to one side, so my head could rest on his shoulder.

"Tom?" I asked, after a few minutes of peace, "You do want me to live with you, don't you?"

"Permanently?"

"Yes."

"I can't think of anything I want more...except for Teddy to come home and be there with us."

That first night was strange. Leaving Teddy's cotside together at the same time in the evening, once I'd sat and expressed enough milk for throughout the night, until I could return in the morning.

The drive home in Tom's car. My hospital bags sitting on the back seat and an overwhelming feeling of emptiness filling me. Is this what Tom had felt like leaving the hospital every day?

"I don't think I can do this," I'd mumbled, when the car pulled out of the carpark. Tom had reached over and taken my hand in his, squeezing it gently. He didn't need to ask what I meant.

Entering his quiet flat, it looked almost unlived in, despite Tom sleeping there each night. He'd not cooked a meal there in almost two weeks, and when we entered the living room the same books were scattered across the coffee table that had been there the last time I was.

"Where's Buddy?" I'd completely forgotten about Tom's lovely little doggy.

"He's with my sister, I've popped by a couple of times. She'll look after him for as long as we need her too," Tom explained, once he'd deposited my bags in the bedroom.

"I'll have need of him soon, he gives the best snuggles."

"Give it a few more days," Tom smiled, and then knelt down and helped me take my shoes off. When he stood up to face me, he asked, "Are you hungry? I don't have much in, but I could order something?"

"I don't know, I'm really tired. I could kill for a bath also... but I am hungry."

"How about, I run you a nice bath, and whilst you're in there, I'll order us some pizza. Then we can have it in bed?"

"You're going to allow food in the bed?"

"For you, darling," he teased.

The Bath felt incredible. After a fortnight of showers, and sleeping on a hard hospital bed, and reclining chairs at my baby's cot side, a bath did wonders to relieve me of all the muscle aches.

However, I'd not completely thought it through. I'd managed to get myself into the bath, very slowly and carefully, I must add. I'd also managed washing my hair and completing all my other ablutions without issue. But I couldn't get out of the bath.

I was stuck. Stuck and mortified.

I'd attempted to push myself up from my seated position, but between the lack of strength in my arms and my still sore scar on my lower belly, I'd sploshed back down in the water very quickly. Then I'd rethought my actions and attempted to wiggle around and get onto my knees. But it wasn't a huge bath and I couldn't twist my body in the right way, without causing myself incredible pain.

I must have sat, contemplating my next move for a full ten minutes before Tom's voice sounded through the bathroom door.

"Are you alright, Ada. You've been a long time in there."

"I..." I paused, realising that I was going to have to ask for his help, "I can't get out the bath."

Tom didn't ask if he could come in or wait for my invitation. The door opened, and he walked in. "Why on earth didn't you ask me for help?"

"Because erm...well..." I trailed off, realising I'd automatically wrapped my arms around my chest to cover myself, and had my legs pressed tightly together. Tom was yet to see my post pregnancy body. I hadn't even looked at it properly, due to a lack of mirrors in hospital. I'd never been body conscious until now, I'd always quite proud of what I had. But now I was painfully aware of the still fresh scar just above my bikini line, red and swollen from the infection, and mottled bruising all around it. Then there were my boobs, which in size were akin to two huge watermelons attached to my chest. They looked utterly ridiculous and felt uncomfortable and heavy. Looking down at them, I could see angry red stretch marks, and visible blue veins covering my pale mounds. Then there were my nipples. They'd darkened throughout pregnancy, but now they were surrounded by a larger, almost brown areola and the buds themselves were red, and big, and constantly hard from regular pumping. I let out a long, resigned sigh, and admitted, "I didn't want you to see me whilst I look like this."

"Like what?"

"This," I lifted one hand and gestured up and down my form.

"Ada, why would you think you would ever need to hide your body from me?" Tom approached the bath and knelt beside me, concern in his eyes.

"Because my body is different now, and not in a good way. My stomach still looks gross and my boobs...oh god. They're horrible, they're ruined!" I wasn't upset, I just felt angry. I wasn't used to feeling this way, and that alone made me feel guilty for being vein.

"Your stomach will heal and your boobs...are magnificent, Ada."

"You've not seen them uncovered, they look like over inflated beach balls."

"They're magnificent because they are making the milk which our son is thriving on. You'll get your body back, darling. But you're still beautiful, you know how gorgeous I think you are. Even more so now because every mark on your body is a reminder that you grew our baby boy," Tom reached out and brushed my wet hair from where it had stuck to my cheeks and tucked it behind my ears. "Now shall we get you out of there?"

It wasn't an easy feat. Lot's of hissing, and yelping on my part, and apologies rushing from Tom's lips, but eventually I was standing and carefully stepping out of the bath, and onto the mat. I didn't miss, when I was finally steady on my feet, Tom's eyes darkening, as they swept up and down my body. That was all I needed to put my insecurities to bed. Even in this state, he still wanted me.

It was when Tom fetched a towel off the side, I was suddenly aware of a warm trickling sensation on the lower half of my breasts, "Fuck!"

Tom spun round with my towel in hand, to see me with my hands covering my nipples, and my cheeks beet red, "What? Are you okay?"

"Erm…I need to pump. Now," the hot bath, and perhaps the brief flood of arousal had triggered my let down reflex and warm milk was flowing freely from my breasts. Tom didn't hesitate to wrap the towel around my body, the flannel immediately soaking up the moisture, and he ushered me through the flat to the bedroom and sat me down on the edge of the bed. Then he was rummaging through my bags fetching out my cow milking contraption.

My first true glimpse of life as a mother came before my baby was even home. Tom and I sat on the bed, pizza boxes open in front of us. Me with a slice of pizza in one hand and holding my breast pump in place with the other.

CHAPTER TWENTY

It's all coming together

It's funny, when your life goes off piste and you find yourself settling into a little routine with it. A bit like when you go on a two week all inclusive holiday, and for a period you find a sense of normality takes over.

The next six weeks, my normality was eight o'clock starts, breakfast at home, Tom's home. Then we would head to the hospital. Tom had to return to work, but only three days a week, so some mornings he would drop me outside the hospital, other days he would come with me. The days he had work, he would always come straight to the ward when he finished. We would stay until early evening, usually just after the nurses had done their night shift hand over. Then we'd go home, and eat dinner, and go to bed.

Throughout the day, we settled into parenthood in the safe-haven of the hospital. We could change nappies now and hold him whenever we wanted to. We could even bath him. But he was still very small, and very weak.

Teddy was around six weeks old when he successfully latched to my breast for the first time. He'd been suckling on a little dummy for a couple of weeks, which taught him the motion he would need to take my milk, but also train him to breathe through his nose whilst feeding. It took several attempts, and it was frustrating and sometimes upsetting. But finally, one afternoon, when I was sitting alone on the ward, and he was fussing for food, I calmly picked him up and put him to my breast. He'd nuzzled, and searched for a moment, little mouth straining open trying to work out where the smell was coming from, then he figured it out.

I'd held my breath for a second. It wasn't the first time he'd almost got there, but it had always been a poor latch and he'd let go quickly, becoming too hungry, upset and frustrated to try again. But this time I could feel it was a good latch. It didn't hurt, and I could feel the milk flowing and see his little throat moving as he guzzled it down.

It was all up from there.

"I just think, what with Tom working so much, it would be a good idea for you and Teddy to stay with us for a little while," my Mum was holding Teddy, bouncing him gently in her arms, "Its hard enough as it is having a baby at home for the first time."

"I'm capable of looking after him alone, Mum," I rolled my eyes. I was fed up with this argument. Although Dena had come around to the idea, and slowly she was becoming more civil with Tom. He and Matt were even on regular speaking terms again, everyone still felt my decision to take Teddy home to Tom's would be a mistake.

"I just don't think you realise how much stress a baby can put on a relationship. Things are still new with the pair of you."

"I want to be with Tom, Tom wants to be with me. This whole ordeal has put an enormous amount of pressure on us, and we are only growing stronger. How can you tell me that Teddy and I would be better off apart from him?"

"I'm not saying –" but my Mum's counter argument was cut off.

"I hope I'm not interrupting," I balked at the voice behind me, and turned to see Ms. Susan Cambridge, giving me her usual stink-eye.

"No of course not," I said quickly. I was probably trying too hard. I was doing all I could to help smooth over the relationship between Tom and his Mum. I'd even made a point of making myself scarce when she visited so she could spend time with her grandson, without concerning herself with me. But today I hadn't expected her. "Please come in," I waved her into Teddy's bay, "Sit down."

"I think I'm going to go," my Mum couldn't even look at Susan, whilst I scooped my baby from her arms, and pecked her on the cheek to wish her goodbye. My Mum disappeared off the ward and I turned back to Susan, expelling a little huff. She remained quiet and I could feel her eyes on me, whilst I walked in small circles still bouncing Teddy gently in my arms.

"I erm…" I came to a stop in front of her, "Would you like to hold him, he's not long had a feed, so he's quite blissed out at the moment."

"I'd love to, you know I've not held him yet," she looked delighted that I'd offered, and I wondered for a moment if, Tom had not offered her the chance to bond with her grandson yet. He was quite cross, and although he hadn't stopped her visiting, that was only because I insisted that he didn't. Carefully I placed Teddy in her waiting arms, his tiny head resting in the crook of her elbow, she tucked him close to her body, and simply stared at him. If I wasn't mistaken I was certain I saw a few tears trickle down her cheeks. "Would you like a drink? I can go grab one from the family lounge?"

"Oh, it should be me doing that!" She glanced up.

"Seriously, I spend so many hours sitting in this one spot, that a jaunt to the lounge is a welcome break," I chuckled, "Tea?"

She nodded, "Milky, and one sugar. Thank you."

When I returned with two cups of tea, I was in time to see Susan placing Teddy in his cot. He was sound asleep now. Snoring softly, I always knew he was well away when he snored.

"He sounds like Tom," Susan commented with a little smile, when I placed her drink on the table next to her.

"I always tease him about that."

"I overheard the conversation with your Mum... about Teddy going home."

"Ah...yes," I tried not to groan, sure I was about to get another lecture.

"I admire you standing your ground. You've not been well, I appreciate that. It's so easy to let people push you around and make decisions for you when you're not feeling your best."

"The only person who listens to me is Tom."

"I've been terrible to you...I've made judgements of you and I've behaved out of character. I have no reasonable excuse, except... I just wanted someone else to blame for my son's behaviour," Susan sighed loudly, and almost fell back into her chair, but she looked up at me, her expression somewhat desperate.

"Tom's behaviour…he's made mistakes. But every single one of those mistakes he's made, whilst trying desperately to do right by everyone," my knee jerk reaction was to jump to my boyfriend's defence.

"I know that, Ada. I do know that. Tom is a good man," she stopped, screwing up her face and shaking her head, "But unfortunately, I care far too much what people think. I'm cross with him, because his behaviour has lead to situation which wouldn't be an unusual on a popular, ITV daytime talk show. But it doesn't happen in my family. His father and I paid to put him through the best education possible…he's a Doctor!"

"Doctor's make mistakes too," I interjected, "And my Dad's a famous music producer, we have friends in high places. But my family aren't worrying what people think, or slagging off Tom for knocking me up!"

"This isn't just about Teddy, but everything before…with Grace."

"Oh…" to be honest, I'd not considered the Grace situation. It felt like a lifetime ago now. A situation that Tom sorted, and to my knowledge he'd not heard a word from her since the sale of their house went through almost five months ago. She'd gone back to America and that was that.

"Tom falls fast and heavy. He always has, I thought he might grow out of it…but he hasn't. Grace was a prime example, he threw his life into that relationship, and even when he found out she was pregnant with another man's child he stood by her, he didn't want to lose her. I personally don't believe Grace ever intended to stay with Tom, she got what she needed from him. Did he ever tell you? I doubt he has…half the house. His house, he put her name on the mortgage, biggest mistake he ever made," Susan shook her head.

"He got taken for a ride?" I hadn't realised. And she was right, Tom had never told me. It made sense though. Why he was so apprehensive to involve himself with me. Why he wanted to ensure he was financially providing for me and the baby. How humiliated he must have felt, how used. But he never let on, not once.

"I was scared, Ada. When I saw you...you are so unlike any woman Tom had ever been in a relationship with. I judged you for the way you look, which... I admit, I'm not fond of...all the tattoos and the hair," she gestured at me vaguely, she wasn't being nasty, just honest, "Your appearance does not reflect upon your heart, your intellect, or your ability to be a good mother. I'm ashamed of speaking of you, and to you the way I did."

"I understand."

"Do you?"

"I'm so different from anyone you've known, my whole family are a little... different. You didn't know me, and you were scared Tom was being taken advantage of. That he'd just got swept away again—"

She stopped me, "But I didn't try to know you, that's the point. I saw you and jumped to all the worst conclusions. What's worse is you were so poorly, and so was Teddy. I should have been supporting my son, he was distraught."

"I adore him."

"I don't doubt it," Susan smiled sincerely at me, "And I honestly think for the first time, Tom may have met a woman who is just as invested in the relationship as he is. I've thought a lot about that day, how you stood up to me. Even now, you defend him, relentlessly. You truly believe the safest most, secure place for you and Teddy to be is with Tom."

"It is, he's Teddy's Dad, it's the only place both of us should be, and the only place I want to be."

"I hope, you can forgive me, Ada, and when Teddy is home, and settled, I can have an opportunity to get to know you properly."

*

I sat curled up at the end of the sofa. Teddy attached to my breast, suckling away happily. Buddy curled up on my feet. He never strayed too far away from me or Teddy. The television played quietly with the six o'clock news. But I wasn't really playing attention. I was practically falling asleep.

Although I was jerked awake when I heard the jingle of keys in the front door. Buddy's head stuck up to acknowledge his Daddy's return home, but he didn't move from his spot, choosing instead to lick my toes.

"We're in here," I called out from the lounge, and Tom appeared in the room second later. I gave him a sleepy smile.

"How are my two favourite people today?" Tom asked as he leant over and pushed a kiss to the top of my head, then ducked down further and brushed his lips over Teddy's soft little head. His hair was longer now and curling at the ends. It was also a very distinct shade of red.

"Hmm, tired," I hummed.

Teddy had been home from hospital for one whole week. Contrary to my family and Dena's reservations, I was coping extraordinarily well. The first night, I'd been so terrified of Teddy waking and me not hearing him, that I couldn't sleep. But with lots of assurance from Tom, that he was right next to us, we would most definitely hear him, and echoing the doctor's words that my milk would let me know before Teddy, when I needed to wake to feed him, I soon calmed down.

Now, seven days later we'd even managed to find some semblance of a routine. Even Dena had admitted I'd made the right choice, and she absolutely loved that Teddy and I were just five minutes around the corner from her. She'd already been round almost every single day after work.

"I'll sort dinner if you'd like?" Tom offered, like he did every single day.

"I've done it, there's a casserole in the oven," Tom shook his head.

"You're too good, darling," He shrugged off his jacket, and untied his scarf, throwing them both over the back of the arm chair. The sight of him, all tousled from the wind, and cheeks red from the cold filled me with warmth. I loved the calm domesticity we'd found. "Buddy, off," Tom pointed at the floor, and spoke to his dog with a firm voice. But as usual, Buddy ignored the very simple instruction.

"He's on the blanket," I defended my furry friend. That was the agreement, since Buddy refused to leave my side when I tended to Teddy, that he could sit on the sofa as long as he was on the blanket.

"Yes, but I want to catch a snuggle as well, Daddy needs some Mummy time," Tom pouted.

"You'll get plenty of Mummy time later. Now you can burp this one, whilst I dish up dinner," I replied cheekily. I smiled fondly as Teddy's head lolled to one side, milk drunk. I tucked myself away and stood up, handing the tiny infant over to Tom. I was sure to lean up and catch his mouth in a kiss as I did.

"I'll hold you to that, sweetheart," Tom chuckled, as I looked back with a flirty wink, and left to serve dinner.

CHAPTER TWENTY-ONE

It started with a wedding

"I think green was a good choice, I like it," I could hear Dena in the next room, her voice above everyone else's. "It's so pretty, isn't it? Festive!"

"Well, I think that was the point Dena," my Mum was speaking now, "What with it being Yuletide."

"Well I know," there was a knock at the door, "Oh that'll be Natalie with the girls!"

I should probably make an appearance. I'd been hiding out in the bedroom, feeling so overwhelmed by Dena and my Mother in the same room, along with Tom's oldest sister Amelia, who I'd only met once before, and soon the arrival of Natalie, his other sister and her two daughters. My gaggle of Bridesmaids.

I was getting married, and that in its self was overwhelming, and it had all happened so quickly. Dena's repeated excitable outbursts over the past few months of 'I can't believe you're getting married!' echoed in my head now. I couldn't believe it either.

The venue was idyllic. I'd never given much thought to what sort of wedding I'd like, and upon getting engaged I hadn't been the over enthused bride everyone expected me to be. I had breathed an audible sigh of relief when my Dad told me he would arrange a wedding planner. But now I stood staring out of the floor to ceiling window of the beautiful country retreat that was Buxted Park in Sussex. I knew I'd have never been able to choose such a perfect location for our guests to enjoy our day with us.

Because that was the thing. This wasn't for us, not really. I know I'd have been happy popping down the town hall and I'm sure, knowing Tom how I do, as long as the day ended with us wed, he wouldn't care where, when or how it took place.

But just like everything between Tom and I, it just sort of happened, and it happened quickly. Teddy was now just over a year old. This contributed to my hesitance to plan a huge wedding. I didn't want to take away from that important first year of my Son's life. We could have waited, and had a long engagement, but from the second Tom proposed, and I said yes, we both knew neither of our families would stand for that. And honestly, I couldn't wait to be his wife either.

But even the engagement had sort of come out of the blue and very quickly.

Teddy had come home from hospital in early December. Just in time for Christmas. Tom's proposal came on Christmas day. Although it wasn't meant to, he hadn't planned to propose at all. He'd not even brought a ring.

With Teddy still being so young, and it being hard enough having a new born, without traipsing around the country visiting family, we'd told everyone if they wanted to see us at Christmas, they would need to come to us, but we wouldn't be cooking.

Christmas day ended up just being the three of us, we got a Chinese take away, and snuggled up together watching movies. We both agreed it was one of the best Christmas' we'd ever had.

"I want to spend every Christmas like this," Tom had been snuggled to my side, arm firmly wrapped around my mid-section, head tucked on my shoulder.

"Hmm, me too," I'd agreed sleepily, pressing my lips to the top of his head, cushioned by his silky curls. I giggled as they tickled my nose, then he tipped his head back, so I could kiss his lips.

A few beats of silence passed, "Why don't we then?"

"Huh?"

"Why don't we spend every Christmas like this? Together?"

"Well I don't intend on spending it with anyone else," but I was still clueless as to where Tom was going with this conversation.

"No, Ada," he finally pushed himself up and took my hands in his, drawing my attention to him completely. I shuffled myself around so I was facing him. "I'm asking you to spend your life with me, to be my wife."

"Yes."

"Yes?"

"Yes, Tom, of course I'll marry you, you doughnut!"

"Oh!"

"Did you think I was going to say no?"

"I have no idea," then he laughed, pulling me a little roughly into his arms, "I didn't even know I was going to ask!"

"Well, then maybe I should be asking if you're sure want to marry me?"

That was that, we were engaged. But then nothing happened for a little while. We told our families when they visited in the days that followed. I nearly caused Dena to choke on her own tongue when I mentioned it in passing.

It wasn't until several weeks later that Tom took me to a jeweller and we chose a ring together. An over the top, far too expensive eighteen carat, double halo set, diamond ring. Tom insisted I chose what I really liked and wanted, not what I deemed sensible or practical. I'd never been a sensible and practical sort of girl, and let's face it, although I may not have been over-enthusing about planning a wedding…Diamonds were a girl's best friend.

Once I had the ring, that's when Dena, my Mother and even Susan started. My mother pleaded with me not to drag out the engagement and even Tom asked me more than once a week if I wanted to start looking at venues and thinking about dates. Eventually, I'd lost my temper with him, and told him I didn't have time to plan a wedding, and he and everyone else would just have to wait until Teddy was a bit older.

Three days later my Dad called and told me he'd arranged the wedding planner. Tom didn't even try to pretend he had nothing to do with it. He'd blatantly got my parents on side. But he was Tom, and he could do very little wrong in my eyes. How could I be angry that he wanted to marry me, and he didn't want to wait.

Christmas was Susan's idea. Not Christmas day, but just a couple of days before. My Dad suggested the venue, and my Mum had dealt with the decoration. Tom decided on everything else.

My involvement went as far as the colour scheme and my dress.

My dress was gorgeous. I knew Dena was quite jealous she'd not seen it first. A stunning Ivory A-Line gown, with applique detailing on the upper bodice, and then stitched along the train. It sat just off the shoulders, and had a sweetheart neckline, enhancing my already generous bust. I think my Mum had expected a slightly more unusual design, but it complimented my style nonetheless.

I let out a long shaky breath. I wasn't nervous though. Just... overwhelmed. I never, in a million years thought I'd be a bride. But looking in the mirror now, that was me, with a veil, and the dress which made me look like a princess.

"Holy Fuck, I'm getting married," I muttered to myself, before picking up my glass of champagne and taking draining the rest of it.

"Holy Fuck indeed."

"Jesus, Dena!" I'd not heard her come in.

"Feeling religious today, are we?"

"You're hilarious."

"You look stunning," if she'd told me once, she'd told me a thousand times. Just as I had her, on her special day. The day I met Tom for the first time.

"So, do you," she'd changed into her Bridesmaid's dress. A forest green swing dress, with a scalloped low-cut neckline and baroque detailing all over. I couldn't wait to see Amelia and Natalie in theirs.

"Natalie's here with the girls, they look adorable!" She squeaked a little, "And Matt just sent me a picture of Ted in his little suit, he's so, so cute, Ada!"

"How long do I have?" I glanced around for a clock.

"About twenty minutes, but the photographer wants to get a few photos of us girls all together before you go," Dena explained, "Are you nervous?"

"No!" I answered quickly.

"Then what the bloody hell is the matter with you? You were all smiles and joy this morning! It's your wedding day!"

"Don't laugh," I warned, a smile suddenly finding my lips, "I miss Tom."

"Eh?"

"I miss him, and Teddy. But yeah... I just got really overwhelmed, so I came in here for a little bit of space and started thinking about everything and how lucky I am to have him. I just love him so much, and I never thought I'd want to get married. But now... there's nothing I want more, and it's so crazy and fast and it doesn't feel real," I stopped for breath, then launched back into it, "And I know I only saw him yesterday morning, but that's already too long, and I honestly don't know how I won't pick up my dress and sprint down that aisle when I see him."

When I finally finished, Dena was beaming at me. "That's what it's meant to feel like, you silly girl! Now come on, everybody's waiting!"

Tom's sisters fussed over me, the moment they saw me. Natalie had become somewhat of a friend. She only lived about a half an hour bus ride away and being a mother of two, I'd found myself turning to her frequently for advice. She only worked a few hours a week, so we'd take the children to the park sometimes, or go for coffee.

Amelia, I'd met once before in person, but Tom Skyped her at least once a week, and I'd spoken to her many times. She visited a few weeks before the wedding for her dress fitting, and so we could meet properly before the big day. She was more like Tom than Natalie, both in looks and temperament, and we'd hit it off immediately.

Just a Dena had said, Tom's two young nieces looked adorable. They wore little Ivory flower girl dresses with forest green sashes tied at the waist. I dropped to my knees and made a big fuss of them, telling them how beautiful and grown up they both looked.

My Dad cried when he saw me. I hadn't been prepared for his emotional outburst and in turn I cried, then I had my make-up artist flapping around trying to make sure my eyeliner hadn't smudged, and I didn't have tracks in my airbrushed foundation.

But finally, after twenty minutes of fussing, photos and touch ups, a knock came on the door. It was the wedding co-ordinator, Lisa, telling us they were ready for me.

"Your man looks very handsome," Lisa told me, as we walked down the hallways, my arm was linked through my Dad's. Dena was just ahead of us with Natalie, Amelia and the girls. My Mum had gone further ahead to take her seat. "He can't wait to see you, are you excited?"

I just nodded. Her words were going in one ear and out the other. All I could think about was that in just a few moments I'd be in Tom's arms, and that's where I planned to stay for the rest of my life.

"Ada," my Dad nudged me, "Are you alright? I've never known you so quiet."

"I just want to see Tom."

"He's a very lucky Man, Ada."

"I know he's not the sort of man you envisioned me marrying..." we'd come to a stop and the co-ordinator had rushed forward to get the girls in place. So, I took the very brief moment I had to speak to my Dad. To tell him something I'd been wanting to say for a long time. Although my family liked Tom well enough, my Dad had struggled to get on with him like he had Magnus. There was not a natural rapport and I could tell they both found it hard work to hold conversation together. "But he is a good man, I hope you know that. I hope you can see how well he takes care of me and Teddy."

"Ada, I don't know where you've got this notion that I had a set idea about the kind of man I wanted you to marry," Dad stopped and frowned at me.

"You loved Magnus."

"I did, until he broke my little girl's heart," I couldn't help but smile at this, I'd always be my Dad's little girl. "But you and Magnus were never going to get married, were you?"

"No," I shook my head, "That was never on the agenda."

"So, why do you want to marry Tom? What's different?"

"I love him," I answered without hesitation. But then realised that it sounded like I'd never loved Magnus. I had, of course. "I mean...what I feel with Tom is just...so intense. I need to marry him, not because I think I need to prove our love, but because it feels like this significant step, from one life into a new one, which I'll share with Tom."

"And that's exactly the reason you should be getting married. Because you want to bind yourself to him, sharing your commitment to one another in the presence of your loved ones. It truly is significant," then to my surprise, my Dad leant in and kissed my cheek, "For the record, I think you and Tom are perfect for one another. I can see in the way he looks at you, how he watches you. It's how I see your Mum."

"Thanks, Dad."

"Now come on, let's get you married!"

Lisa hurried about, positioning my flower girls, then Natalie and Amelia, and finally Dena in front of me. Dad and I hung back, just out of sight. I heard the music start up. Okay so I'd had a little play in that as well. I'd composed the music for the ceremony myself, primarily because I'd spent eight months on maternity leave, and I was going mad not working. So, whilst Teddy napped, I'd started tinkling about on my keyboard, then on my computer. The result was a gentle piano piece, beautifully simple in its composition, but also lifting and romantic. I'd not let Tom hear it, as I wanted it to be a surprise. I couldn't wait to see his face, although right now I wasn't sure he'd be focusing on the music, not if he was feeling anything like me.

As Dena was given her nod to walk in behind my other bridesmaids, she glanced over and took a final look at me. She let out a tiny squeak of excitement and beamed at me, before turning and starting her procession.

Then it was my turn. The doors into the Orangery where the ceremony was taking place, were closed temporarily and Dad lead me to stand in front of them. Lisa and another woman stood by both doors, ready for my entrance, she nodded at me, and I gave a little nod back.

I took a big gulp of air, my grip on my Dad's elbow tightening with anticipation. As I released my breath slowly, the doors opened before us.

The room was full, but I could only see Tom.

It was like the air had left the room, silence filled my ears and everything around me vanished, except for the man who stood at the other end of the aisle, his smile widening the closer I got.

He looked incredible. I didn't really note his outfit until I was practically in front of him. A perfectly tailored, double breasted burgundy suit. Despite him normally wearing contacts for special occasions, he had his glasses on, and I noticed immediately that he'd had a hair and beard trim. But his beautiful auburn curls remained, neatly brushed back, but curling at the nape of his neck, just how I liked it.

How I stopped myself tearing away from my Dad and throwing myself into Tom's arms I don't know. But somehow, as I reached my future husband, I allowed myself to turn back to Dad, so he could peck my cheek and hand me over to Tom.

Tom's hands closed around mine when I turned back to him, and his eyes were twinkling when I looked into them. The room was suddenly coming back to me, the music fading out, and Teddy's little voice caught my attention. I glanced over to where he sat on Susan's knee, reaching out in my direction, babbling away because he could see his Mummy. I gave him a little wave, and he squealed and bounced with excitement, drawing a chuckle from our guests. I looked back to Tom.

"Hi," he murmured.

"Hello."

"You look…I don't even have words. I'm so lucky."

I squeezed both of his hands tightly, "So am I. I missed you so much, I love you!"

"I love you, too."

A cough from next to us, drew our attention to the registrar, who looked suitably guilty for interrupting our little moment.

"We'll begin," Tom and I nodded, and grinned at each other again, not letting go of the other's hands. "Welcome, family, friends and loved ones. We gather here today to celebrate the wedding of Tom and Ada. You have come here to share in this formal commitment they make to one another, to offer your love and support to this union…"

22978183R00154

Printed in Great Britain
by Amazon